Lend me a tenor : a comedy / by Ken Ludwig

DATE DUE

Lend Me a
TENOR

Lend Me a *Tenor*

A Comedy by
KEN LUDWIG

GARDEN CITY, NEW YORK

Photographs Copyright © 1989 by Martha Swope
Design by Maria Chiarino
Manufactured in the United States of America

Quality Printing and Binding by:
Orange Graphics
P.O. Box 791
Orange, VA 22960 U.S.A.

LEND ME A TENOR was presented at the Royale Theatre in New York City on March 2, 1989, by Martin Starger and Andrew Lloyd Webber for The Really Useful Company. The director was Jerry Zaks; the setting was by Tony Walton; the costumes were by William Ivey Long; the lighting was by Paul Gallo; the production stage manager was Steven Beckler; the stage manager was Clifford Schwartz; the assistant to the director was Lori Steinberg; the general manager was Robert Kamlot; the music coordinator was Edward Strauss; the sound was by Aural Fixation; and the hair was by Angela Gari. The cast was as follows:

MAX	Victor Garber
MAGGIE	J. Smith-Cameron
SAUNDERS	Philip Bosco
TITO	Ron Holgate
MARIA	Tovah Feldshuh
BELLHOP	Jeff Brooks
DIANA	Caroline Lagerfelt
JULIA	Jane Connell

LEND ME A TENOR was previously presented by Andrew Lloyd Webber for The Really Useful Company at the Globe Theatre, London, on March 6, 1986. The director was David Gilmore; the setting and costumes were by Terry Parsons; the lighting was by Michael Northen; the stage manager was Peter Gardner; and the music coordinator was Rod Argent. The cast was as follows:

MAX	Denis Lawson
MAGGIE	Jan Francis
SAUNDERS	John Barron
TITO	Ron Holgate
MARIA	Anna Nicholas
BELLHOP	Edward Hibbert
DIANA	Gwendolyn Humble
JULIA	Josephine Blake

The play was first presented at the American Stage Festival in Milford, New Hampshire, on August 1, 1985. The director was Larry Carpenter; the setting was by John Falabella; the costumes were by David Murin; the lighting was by John Gisondi; and the music coordinator was John Clifton. The cast was as follows:

MAX	Walter Bobbie
MAGGIE	Christine Rose
SAUNDERS	George Ede
TITO	Ron Holgate
MARIA	Judith Roberts
BELLHOP	Joe Palmieri
DIANA	Linda Lee Johnson
JULIA	Bella Jarrett

CHARACTERS

Max . . . . assistant to Saunders
Maggie . . . . Max's girlfriend
Saunders . . . . . Maggie's father, General Manager of the
    Cleveland Grand Opera Company
Tito Merelli . . . . a world famous tenor, known also to his fans
    as Il Stupendo
Maria . . . . his wife
Bellhop . . . . a bellhop
Diana . . . . a soprano
Julia . . . . Chairman of the Opera Guild

The action takes place in a hotel suite in Cleveland, Ohio, in
1934.

ACT ONE

Scene 1

An elegant suite in a first-rate hotel in Cleveland, Ohio. Early afternoon on a Saturday in September, 1934.

Two rooms: a sitting room Stage Right and a bedroom Stage Left with a connecting door that swings open into the bedroom. Up Center in each room is a door to the corridor. In the sitting room, a large window (facing a street, several stories below) and a door to the kitchenette. In the bedroom, two more doors, both along the outside wall, one (upstage) to the closet, the other (downstage) to the bathroom. Six doors in all.

The furniture consists, at a minimum, of a sofa, pouf, radio and coffee table in the sitting room; and a bed and bureau in the bedroom.

As the house lights go down, we hear music: a recording of "La donna e mobile" from Verdi's Rigoletto, *sung thrillingly by a world-class tenor.*

When the lights come up, MAGGIE, *late twenties, pretty and quirky, is alone onstage, sitting on the pouf in the sitting room. She listens rapturously to the music which by now is coming from the radio (and now sounds scratchy as on an old recording). She is entirely caught up in the sensual sound of the tenor's voice. She sways to the music and mouths the words.*

After several seconds, MAX, *mid-thirties and rumpled, enters the sitting room from the corridor. He wears glasses. He also wears a scarf, indicating that he's just been outdoors. He enters hurriedly, with urgency.*

He looks around the room, confirming in an instant that TITO *isn't there.*

MAX *(over the music)*: Maggie—!

MAGGIE: Shhh!

MAX: Did he call?!

MAGGIE: No. Now will you wait!

(MAX *sighs. He looks at his watch. Then he notices* MAGGIE's *reaction to the music; she's swaying in rapture. The aria ends and* MAGGIE *falls backward)*

RADIO ANNOUNCER: The magnificent voice of Tito Merelli, brought to you in honor of his live appearance this evening with the Cleveland Grand Opera Company—

(MAX *turns off the radio)*

MAX: He wasn't on the train.

MAGGIE: Oh my God. He is so wonderful. When he does that last note, I almost can't breathe.

MAX: Maggie, he wasn't there! *(The phone rings.* MAX *grabs it)* Hello?! . . . No, sir, I couldn't find him.

SAUNDERS *(through the phone): Goddammit! Where the hell is he?!*

MAX *(to* MAGGIE): It's your father. *(Into the phone)* I don't know! I looked everywhere. I asked the conductor. I had him paged. I— I—I'm sorry, I just—

(The sound of SAUNDERS *hanging up)*

MAX: Sir? . . . Sir? (MAX *hangs up)* He's gonna kill me.

MAGGIE: He will not. He'd have nobody to yell at. At least nobody who takes it the way you do.

MAX: Maggie, the man is two hours late! The rehearsal starts in *ten minutes!*

MAGGIE: He'll be here, Max. This is Tito Merelli. He's a genius. They just don't think like other people.

MAX: So what are you saying? He's a grown man and he can't tell time?

MAGGIE: I'm just not worried, okay? *(Pause)* Oh, Max, just think of it. Tonight. The curtain rises and he walks onstage. And suddenly there's nothing else in the world but that . . . that *voice.*

(Pause)

MAX: I can sing too, you know.

MAGGIE: Oh, Max—*(She laughs out loud)*

MAX: I can! What are you—"Oh, Max."

MAGGIE: You don't sing like Tito Merelli.

MAX: Not yet. Okay?

MAGGIE: You don't.

MAX: In your opinion. It's a matter of taste.

MAGGIE: It is not! I wish you wouldn't fool yourself. He's a star, Max. He sings all over the world. He's in *Life* magazine!

MAX: So is Rin Tin Tin.

MAGGIE: And he's very sensitive.

MAX: How do you know that?

(Beat. She realizes she's caught)

MAGGIE *(casually):* Because I met him. Last year.

MAX: You did? You never told me that.

MAGGIE: It was no big thing. When I was in Italy with Daddy, we went to La Scala and he was in *Aida.* Then afterwards we went backstage and . . . well, there he was, all by himself, behind the curtain. He was wearing a sort of . . . loincloth and his whole body was pouring with sweat. Anyway, he looked up and saw us and do you know what he did, Max. He kissed my palms.

MAX: Yeah? So what?

MAGGIE: It was romantic.

MAX: He's Italian! They kiss everything!

MAGGIE: Fine, forget it.

MAX: If it moves they kiss it.

MAGGIE: Max!

MAX: So what else happened?

MAGGIE: Nothing. *(Pause)* Of any importance.

MAX: Something else happened?

MAGGIE: Not really.

MAX: Something sort of happened.

MAGGIE: It wasn't important.

MAX: What happened!

MAGGIE: It was nothing! Oh—! *(Reluctantly; embarrassed)* I fainted.

MAX: You fainted?

MAGGIE: It must have been the heat and all the excitement. I remember thinking suddenly, my God, it's like an oven back here. And we were talking and he sort of . . . stared right at me, and then I . . . blacked out.

MAX: Oh great. I mean this is terrific. My fiancee meets this—this sweaty Italian guy and she keels over.

MAGGIE: From the heat! And I'm not your fiancee, Max.

MAX: Wait a minute. Did I ask you to marry me or not? Huh? Remember that? What did you—you black out during the proposal?

MAGGIE: I heard it, Max, and I said no.

MAX: You said you'd think about it.

MAGGIE *(taking his hand):* Max. I'm just not ready yet. I want something special first. Something wonderful and romantic.

MAX: I'm not romantic? I don't believe this. What do you call a rowboat at three a.m., huh? Moonlight shimmering on the water. Nobody for miles.

MAGGIE: You lost the oars.

MAX: But it was fun! It turned out fun!

MAGGIE: We spent thirty hours in a rowboat, Max.

MAX: That's not the point!

MAGGIE: I haven't had any flings, Max.

MAX: Flings?

MAGGIE: Flings.

MAX: I've been asking you to fling with me for three years! I begged you!

MAGGIE: I don't mean that! I just feel that I need some . . . wider experience.

MAX: Oh. Sure. I get it. You mean like Diana.

MAGGIE: Diana?

MAX: Desdemona. Soprano.

MAGGIE: Oh, her.

MAX: She's flinging her way through the whole cast. All the men are getting flung out. You should see the guy who plays Iago. He's supposed to be evil. He can hardly walk.

MAGGIE: Max—

MAX: He's limping now—

MAGGIE: Max, listen. Let's be honest. When you kiss me, do you hear anything? Special?

MAX: Like what?

MAGGIE: Like . . . bells.

MAX: You wanna hear bells?

MAGGIE: I guess it sounds stupid, doesn't it?

MAX: Yeah. It does.

MAGGIE: Just forget it.

(A knock at the door)

SAUNDERS *(offstage):* Max!

MAX *(torn):* Maggie—

MAGGIE: I said forget it!

(More knocking)

SAUNDERS *(offstage):* Max!

MAX: Coming!

(MAX opens the door and SAUNDERS rushes in. Mid–fifties, authoritarian and very upset)

SAUNDERS: Well? Any word?!

MAX: Not yet.

SAUNDERS: Goddammit!!

MAX: I—I—I'm sorry.

MAGGIE: Max!

SAUNDERS (*to* MAGGIE): What the hell are you doing here?

MAGGIE: I'm sure I can be here if I want to.

SAUNDERS: Wrong.

MAGGIE: Daddy—!

SAUNDERS: Do you know what time it is?

MAX: It's almost one.

SAUNDERS: Do you know what that means?

MAX: He's late.

SAUNDERS: It means he's late!!!

(SAUNDERS *takes a grape from the fruit bowl*)

MAX: I—I wouldn't worry, sir. I mean, I'm sure he'll get here.

SAUNDERS: Do I seem worried, Max?

MAX: No! No.

MAGGIE: Max!

MAX: I mean . . . well . . . yeah. You do.

SAUNDERS: I do? How interesting. In that case, perhaps you can
tell us what extrasensory, Maxian perception has led you to form
this startling and erroneous conclusion.

(He pops the grape in his mouth)

MAX: That . . . that's wax fruit.

(SAUNDERS *blows the grape across the room [into the audience])*

SAUNDERS: Goddammit!!

MAGGIE: Daddy!

MAX: I'm sorry!

SAUNDERS: Call the station!

MAX: I was just there—

SAUNDERS: CALL THE STATION!

MAX: Yes, sir.

(He goes to the phone, finds the phone book and looks for the number)

MAGGIE: Daddy, have you taken your pills?

SAUNDERS: Yes, yes.

MAGGIE: You're lying, Daddy.

(She rummages through her handbag and comes up with a bottle of pills)

SAUNDERS: I am perfectly capable of controlling my own nervous system. Where would Lauritz Melchior be today if he'd taken phenobarbital?

MAGGIE: Open wide.

SAUNDERS: Margaret . . .

MAGGIE: Mouth!

(He sticks out his tongue, she puts the pill on it and he swallows it. The phone rings. They all freeze. Then MAX *reaches for it)*

SAUNDERS: No! He's been in an accident. I can feel it. *(It rings again)* He's lying in the gutter, stinking drunk on cheap Chianti.

(It rings again)

MAGGIE: Max.

SAUNDERS: All right! Pick it up!

(MAX *picks it up)*

MAX *(into the phone):* Hello? . . . Yes it is . . . Oh no. That's terrible.

SAUNDERS: He's dead. Selfish bastard.

MAX *(to* SAUNDERS): It's Mrs. Leverett. The rehearsal's starting.

SAUNDERS: Give me that! *(He grabs the phone. Suddenly charming)* Madam Chairman, how very kind of you to c— . . . No. No, he hasn't quite arrived yet . . . Julia . . . Jul— . . . Juli— . . . Julia! Will you calm down! . . . What? . . . *(He sighs)* . . . I see . . . Well, if I may, I will leave that decision in your capable hands. Right. Goodbye. *(He hangs up)* It appears that the Opera Guild Collation Committee has decided to serve shrimp mayonnaise at the intermission, the refrigerator has broken down and the temperature backstage is a hundred degrees.

MAX: So what do we do?

SAUNDERS: We play it by ear. If the shrimp stays pink, the audience gets it. If it turns green, we feed it to the stagehands.

MAX: Shall I call the station?

SAUNDERS: No. I've changed my mind. I want the line open. *(To* MAGGIE) And I want you out of here.

MAGGIE: Why?

SAUNDERS: Because I said so.

MAGGIE: Daddy!

SAUNDERS: Max and I have some business to discuss.

MAGGIE: I won't say a word.

SAUNDERS: Out.

MAGGIE: I'll wait in the bedroom.

SAUNDERS: Wrong.

MAGGIE: But I want to see him! You said I could. You promised!

SAUNDERS: Well I lied, you nitwit! Now get out!

MAGGIE: Max thinks I should stay. Don't you, Max?

(Pause)

MAX: I—I think he's right.

MAGGIE: I see.

SAUNDERS: Goodbye, my dear.

MAX *(to MAGGIE)*: I'm—I'm sorry.

(MAGGIE *spots the key to the room on the table next to her. Without them seeing it, she picks up the key and takes it with her, with her handbag)*

MAGGIE *(at the door, ignoring MAX)*: See you later . . . Daddy.

(She exits to the corridor, closing the door behind her. MAX *feels like a crumb)*

SAUNDERS: I've got a thousand of Cleveland's so–called cognoscenti arriving at the theatre in six hours in black tie, a thirty–piece orchestra, twenty–four chorus, fifteen stagehands and eight principals. Backstage, I have approximately fifty pounds of rotting shrimp mayonnaise which, if consumed, could turn the Gala Be–A–Sponsor Buffet into a mass murder. All I don't have is a tenor. Time.

MAX: One–fifteen. *(Pause)* I'm—I'm really sorry, sir. I wish there was something I could do to help.

SAUNDERS: It's not your fault, Max. I wish it was. The question now is what to do if that irresponsible Italian jackass doesn't arrive.

MAX: I—I have an idea about that, actually.

SAUNDERS: You do?

MAX: Yeah. I mean, sort of.

SAUNDERS: Well, spit it out, Max.

MAX: The thing is—I mean, I was just—just thinking that—well—I mean—I could do it.

SAUNDERS: Do what?

MAX: Sing it. Otello. Sort of—step in. You see, I—I've been to all the rehearsals and I know the part and I—I mean, I could do it. I know I could.

SAUNDERS: Otello? Big black fellow.

MAX: Yes, sir.

SAUNDERS: Otello, Max. He's huge. He's larger than life. He loves with a passion that rocks the heavens. His jealousy is so terrible that we tremble with irrational fear for our very lives. His tragedy is the fate of tortured greatness, facing the black and gaping abyss of insensible nothingness. It isn't you, Max.

MAX: It—it could be. I mean, if I had the chance.

SAUNDERS *(turning directly front, addressing the audience):* "Ladies and gentlemen. May I have your attention, please. I regret to inform you that Mr. Tito Merelli, the greatest tenor of our generation, scheduled to make his American debut with the Cleveland Grand Opera Company in honor of our tenth anniversary season, is regrettably indisposed this evening, but . . . BUT! . . . I have the privilege to announce that the role of Otello will be sung tonight by a somewhat gifted amateur making his very first appearance on this, or indeed any other stage, our company's very own factotum, gopher and all–purpose dogsbody . . . Max!" Do you see the problem?

MAX: I guess so.

SAUNDERS: Old women would be trampled to death in the stampede up the aisles.

MAX: I see what you mean.

SAUNDERS: Time.

MAX: One–twenty. *(A depressed silence.* SAUNDERS *picks up a grape and starts chewing. Then he realizes and spits it out and starts stamping on it in his fury. Meanwhile, the phone rings.* MAX *picks it up)* Hello? What? Could you speak more slowly, please.

SAUNDERS: If it's Julia, tell her she can take the shrimp and stuff it up her—

MAX *(to* SAUNDERS): Sir! It's him! He's in the lobby!

*(*SAUNDERS *runs to the phone and grabs it.)*

SAUNDERS *(into the phone, all charm):* Signor Merelli! Benvenuto a Cleveland! I will be down immediamente. Presto. *(He hangs up.)* All right, Max. This is it. You have your instructions. Key word, Max.

MAX: Glue.

SAUNDERS: Glue. You will stick to him like

MAX: glue

SAUNDERS: and you will not let him out of your

MAX: sight.

SAUNDERS: You will drive him to the rehearsal and then drive him back. You will give him whatever he wants except

MAX: liquor and women.

SAUNDERS: At the performance, you will lead a spontaneous

MAX: standing ovation

SAUNDERS: then return him to the reception, keeping him

MAX: sober

SAUNDERS: with his hands

MAX: to himself

SAUNDERS: at which point he can

MAX: drop dead

SAUNDERS: for all we care. Good.

MAX: Good.

(Break. SAUNDERS *crosses to the corridor door, pauses)*

SAUNDERS: Max!

MAX: Sir?

SAUNDERS: Get rid of that fruit bowl.

(SAUNDERS *exits, pulling the door closed behind him. Simultaneously,* MAGGIE *enters quickly through the bedroom/corridor door and closes it quietly. Then she darts to the bathroom and enters it, slamming the door behind her in her haste. As* MAX *is entering the kitchenette with the fruit, he hears the door slam and stops, puzzled. Still holding the fruit, he walks into the bedroom and looks around. He opens the closet door. No one there. He goes to the bathroom door, opens it, and* MAGGIE, *who was holding the doorknob inside, is yanked into the room)*

MAX *(horrified):* Maggie!

MAGGIE: Is he here?

MAX: No! But he's coming up!

MAGGIE *(excited):* Oh, Max!

MAX: Maggie, do you realize what this looks like? I mean, waiting for him in the bathroom! *(A knock at the sitting room/corridor door)* He's here!

MAGGIE *(in raptures):* Oh, Max!

MAX: With your father!

MAGGIE: 'Bye, Max.

(She steps back into the bathroom and closes the door)

MAX: Maggie!

SAUNDERS *(offstage):* Ma–ax. The door is *locked,* Max.

MAX: Coming! *(He heads for the sitting room. Stops)* Fruit! *(Which he is still holding. Back to the bathroom)* Maggie! Door!

*(*MAGGIE *comes out, annoyed)*

MAGGIE: Max!

MAX: Fruit! *(He hands it to her)*

MAGGIE *(touched, accepting it):* Thank you, Max.

(She steps back in and MAX *slams the door)*

SAUNDERS *(offstage):* Ma–ax! Open the door, please!

MAX: Coming!

(He rushes into the sitting room, closing the connecting door. At the corridor door he stops abruptly. Adjusts himself. Opens the door. SAUNDERS *enters)*

SAUNDERS *(offstage—then on):* MAX!!

MAX: Hi.

SAUNDERS *(glaring murderously, then smiling broadly):* Thank you.

(He steps aside, permitting MARIA *and* TITO MERELLI *to enter the sitting room.* MARIA *is the Sophia Loren type: busty, proud and excitable.* TITO *is imposing. Both of them speak, not surprisingly, with Italian accents)*

SAUNDERS: My friends, your suite.

MARIA: So are you, I'm a–sure.

(She flings her fur stole at MAX*)*

SAUNDERS: Thank you. I'll make the introductions, shall I? Signora Merelli, whom we did not expect, but could not possibly be more pleased to have with us. And Signor Tito Merelli, who needs no introduction. My assistant, Max.

MARIA: *Ciao.*

TITO *(handing his hat and coat to* MAX*):* How do you do. John.

MAX: Uh, Max.

SAUNDERS *(enunciating):* Max.

TITO: John!

MAX (*shrugging*): He can call me John, if he wants—

MARIA: My husband would like a–the john. He throws up.

(MAGGIE *sticks her head out of the bathroom. During the following, she tiptoes across the bedroom to listen*)

SAUNDERS: Oh, the *john*. Yes of course. Right this way.

TITO: *Grazie.*

(TITO *and* SAUNDERS *head for the john*)

MAX (*to* MARIA): The john. We—we misunderstood, you see, we usually say the *STOP!!!* (MAGGIE *freezes.* SAUNDERS *and* TITO *stop. They haven't entered the bedroom yet, but* TITO *has opened the connecting door partway*) There—there—there's one in the lobby. It's much—much nicer. Cleaner.

SAUNDERS: Are you all right, Max?

MAX: Me? Fine. I just—they've got this terrific bathroom in the lobby. It's incredible.

SAUNDERS: I'm sure that this one is peachy, Max.

MAX: No. No it isn't. Trust me.

TITO: John!

SAUNDERS: This way. I'm awfully sorry.

(SAUNDERS *leads* TITO *into the bedroom by which time* MAGGIE *has caught on and disappears into the closet, closing the door behind her*)

TITO: *Grazie.*

MARIA (*to* MAX): Forgive a–my husband, eh? (*She shouts*) He's a–stupid!

TITO: SHUT UP!

MARIA: SHUT UP A–YOUSELF!

(TITO *enters the bathroom and slams the door. During the following,* SAUNDERS *listens at the bathroom door, concerned*)

MARIA *(to* MAX): He eats a–like a fat a–pig. We have a–food on the train. He eats a–too much. Then we arrive, he wants a–lunch. "Done eat," I tell 'im. "You get a–sick. You wone be happy." He eats a–like a pig. Two plates. Why, eh? Why?! Because he likes a–bosoms.

MAX: Bosoms?

MARIA: He wants a–bosoms. Is that normal? You tell me. Eh?

MAX: Well, it's—it's—it's—I'd say it's unusual.

SAUNDERS *(returning to the sitting room; jovial):* What is so unusual, Max?

MAX: Mr. Merelli, apparently he—he'd like to have bosoms.

SAUNDERS: Well . . . that's wonderful.

MARIA: The waitress—eh?—she leans a–way over. "You wanna seconds?" He likes a–bosoms, he says a–sure. He's not hungry! He wants a–more bosoms.

MAX: Oh.

SAUNDERS: I see. *(A knock at the corridor door)* Excuse me.

(SAUNDERS *opens the door to find the* BELLHOP, *who enters carrying two suitcases and a vanity case. Immediately, he bursts into the famous aria from* The Barber of Seville)

BELLHOP *(singing):*
Largo al factotum
della citta, largo!
La ran la, la ran la,
la ran la, la!

SAUNDERS: Shut up!

BELLHOP: Where is he?!

MAX: Bathroom.

SAUNDERS: Max!

MAX: Sorry.

SAUNDERS: Luggage in the bedroom, thank you.

BELLHOP: Yes, *sir!*

(MAX *leads him to the bedroom*)

SAUNDERS *(to* MARIA): I'm awfully sorry about that. You'd think that people would have better manners.

MARIA: Hey, it's okay. No big deal, eh? It happens a–ten times a day. Phone rings, I pick it up, I get *Pagliacci.* I go to the butcher, he skins a–the chicken, he sings a–me *Carmen.*

(The phone rings)

SAUNDERS *(to* MARIA): Excuse me.

BELLHOP *(singing at bathroom door, through the keyhole):*
Presto a Bottega,
che l'alba e gia, presto—

MAX: Hey!!

SAUNDERS *(into the phone):* Yes? Hello, Julia . . . Yes, he is!

(SAUNDERS *turns his back and during the following, carries on a silent conversation with* JULIA.

As MAX *lays the fur stole and* TITO's *hat and coat on the bed, the* BELLHOP *opens the closet door, revealing* MAGGIE *standing in the doorway. However, he doesn't see her, having turned away to get the suitcases.* MAX, *however, sees her and reacts. Beat.* MAX *slams the door.*

The BELLHOP *looks up, sees that* MAX *has slammed the door and sighs at* MAX *with annoyance. He returns to the closet door and opens it again—again turning away without seeing* MAGGIE. *As he picks up the two suitcases,* MAGGIE *runs out of the closet and hides behind the closet door.*

As the BELLHOP *enters the closet with the suitcases,* MAX *opens the bedroom/corridor door and motions to* MAGGIE *to leave. She sticks her head out from behind the closet door and shakes it "no." As the* BELLHOP *reenters from the closet, she disappears again.*

The BELLHOP *goes to the bed and gathers up the stole, coat and hat —at which point,* MAGGIE *runs around the closet door and back into the closet, slamming the door behind her. This is followed immediately by* MAX *slamming the corridor door. The* BELLHOP *looks at one door, then the other, then at* MAX, *who feigns innocence, as though nothing has happened.*

The BELLHOP *shrugs and walks to the closet with the wraps. He opens the door and* MAGGIE *is standing there. He stares at her for a moment; then wordlessly, he hands her the hat, coat and fur. She nods as if to say "Thank you," and smiles wanly. The* BELLHOP *closes the door on* MAGGIE. *He turns front, dazed; then shrugs and heads for the sitting room. Before leaving the bedroom, however, he stops and gives* MAX *the "thumbs up" and hits him on the arm as if to say "way to go." Then he goes into the sitting room, followed by* MAX, *who closes the connecting door behind him)*

SAUNDERS *(into the phone):* Julia, as soon as possible! . . . No he's fine . . . Julia, he is perfectly all right! . . . Yes!

(As he talks to JULIA, *the* BELLHOP *comes over with his hand out.* SAUNDERS *hands him a coin)*

BELLHOP *(looking at the tip):* He's got to be kidding.

SAUNDERS: Out! Now!

BELLHOP: That's pathetic.

SAUNDERS *(into the phone):* I'm sorry, Julia. We have a bellhop on our hands who is not only rude, but apparently brainless.

BELLHOP: Nice guy.

SAUNDERS *(he hangs up):* I believe you owe this lady an apology.

BELLHOP: I do?

SAUNDERS: I would say so, yes.

BELLHOP: Fine. *(To* MARIA*) Mia signora, mi dispiace. Non volevo disturbarla. Se l'ho offesa, chiedo scusa, chiedo scusa.* [My dear lady, I'm sorry. I did not intend to bother you. If I have offended you, I certainly beg your forgiveness.]

MARIA: *Non e niente, l'assicuro.* [I assure you, it's of no importance.]

BELLHOP: *Grazie, la saluto.*

MARIA: *Ciao.*

(The BELLHOP *gives* SAUNDERS *a look, then exits to the corridor, closing the door behind him)*

MAX: I hope Mr. Merelli is all right.

MARIA: Phh!

(At this point TITO *emerges from the bathroom, holding the fruit bowl, puzzled by it. He looks sick. He puts it on the bureau, then sits on the bed)*

SAUNDERS: I don't suppose this sort of thing affects his singing. I mean, he will go on?

MARIA: You got a–women in the opera?

SAUNDERS: Women? Well yes, of course. Fourteen.

MARIA: He wouldn't miss it, believe me. You know why? Eh? Because he's got a . . . *(She gropes)* . . . a . . . What's a–the word. Starts a–with P.

SAUNDERS: P?

MAX: Pride?

SAUNDERS: Personality?

MARIA: All men, they got this thing. It starts a–small, it gets a–big and it makes a–trouble.

SAUNDERS: P?

MAX: Privates?

MARIA: Passion! He's got a big a–passion!

MAX: Oh.

SAUNDERS: I see.

(TITO *enters the sitting room*)

MAX: Mr. Merelli!

SAUNDERS: Are you all right?

TITO: Me? I'm a–fine. *Perfetto.*

MARIA *(derisively):* Hoo!

TITO: I'm a–okey–dokey. I feel like ten bucks.

MARIA: Look at 'im, eh? He looks a–like a sick dog.

TITO: I'm tip a–top.

MARIA: Liar!

TITO: Shut up!

MARIA: Phh!

TITO: A little stomach. It's nothing. I'm a–fine. A few more minutes, I'm gonna be even better.

SAUNDERS: Better?

MARIA: That's what I thought. I'll get a–you pills.

(She gets up)

TITO *(a familiar argument):* I done take pills.

MARIA: You need a–pills!

TITO: No! I'm a–Merelli! Merelli says a–no!

MARIA: What's a–matter? You got a girl in there?

TITO: Yeah. Sure. I got a girl. In fact, I got two girls. Both a–naked. Go ahead! Look!

MARIA: Some day, you gonna wake up in a–you bed, you gonna be a soprano!

TITO *(to MAX):* Jealousy, eh? Jealousy! It's a–terrible.

MARIA *(overlapping, to SAUNDERS):* In my heart, he makes a–me sick.

TITO *(overlapping):* She's a crazy woman.

MARIA *(overlapping):* Because he's a–stupid. He's got a–no brains.

TITO *(overlapping):* All the time it's a–jealousy, jealousy, jealousy—

MARIA: SHUT UP!

TITO: SHUT UP A–YOUSELF!

(MARIA *slams into the bedroom. Huffing in unison,* TITO *and* MA-RIA *both sit, he on the sofa, she on the bed. During the following,* MARIA *calms herself, then lies on the bed and flips through a copy of* Vogue)

SAUNDERS: So . . . I uh, I don't mean to be pushy, but I really do think we ought to be going.

TITO: Sure. Okay. Thanks a–for everything. See you tonight.

SAUNDERS: No. Sorry. I meant all of us. To the rehearsal.

TITO: Me?

SAUNDERS: Right.

(TITO *considers it)*

TITO: No. No, I done think so. You want the truth, I'm not so good.

SAUNDERS: You're not?

TITO: No.

SAUNDERS: What's the matter?

TITO: I'm a–sick. I eat too much. I'm a–stupid.

SAUNDERS: Signor Merelli. I don't think you understand. You see, I have a hundred people at the theatre. Cento persona. They're waiting for you.

TITO: Hey. You done get it. I'm gonna sing right now, I'm gonna throw up on the soprano.

SAUNDERS: I don't believe this.

TITO: Hey! Done worry, okay? Tonight I'm gonna be there. I'm a–Merelli. I done miss performance.

SAUNDERS: But you don't know the stage directions! The—the tempos!

TITO: I sing Otello fifty times. Is no big deal.

SAUNDERS: And what about the costume fitting?

TITO: I bring a—my own. It's in the suitcase. You wanna see? In fact, I bring a—two costumes. Just in case.

SAUNDERS: You can't do this.

TITO: I wear my own costume at Vienna Staatsoper, Covent Garden. You think in Cleveland I'm gonna suffer?

(The phone rings. SAUNDERS *grabs it)*

SAUNDERS *(into the phone):* Yes? . . . OH MY GOD!!! . . . I'll be right there. Just keep looking! . . . Jul— . . . Juli— . . . JULIA, DON'T PANIC!

(He hangs up)

MAX: Trouble?

SAUNDERS: They lost the music. All of it.

TITO: That's not good.

SAUNDERS: All right, now listen. I want an answer and I want it now. Are you coming or not?

TITO: Not.

SAUNDERS: Right. That's settled. Max!

MAX: Sir?

SAUNDERS: If there's a problem of any kind, I want you to call me. Immediately.

MAX: Yes, sir.

SAUNDERS: I'll be at the theatre.

MAX: Right.

(TITO *groans*)

SAUNDERS: Max!

(He motions for MAX *to join him at the door)*

MAX: Sir?

SAUNDERS: He needs some sleep. Do whatever you have to.

MAX: Yes, sir.

(SAUNDERS *exits.* TITO *leans back on the sofa. He doesn't notice at first that* MAX *is still there. Then he does)*

TITO: You stay here?

MAX: Yes. I—I—I mean if you don't mind.

TITO: Sure. Help a–youself. *(He belches, pats his stomach) Scusi.*

MAX: You really are sick, aren't you?

TITO: It's okay. I'm gonna live. In my village, they got a saying— "Nobody ever dies from a–gas." And believe me, they know.

MAX: Yeah, but—but maybe you should take those pills. I mean, they might help.

TITO: Thanks, a–no. I need sleep, not a–pills. I gotta relax. Take a deep breath. It's not so easy, eh?

MAX: Why not?

TITO: Why not. Today it's a–Cleveland, Monday New York. Rush- ing every place. I live in hotels. I'm gonna have children, they gonna look like bellhops.

MAX: I see.

TITO: I get tense, I feel a–sick—then I can't sing nothing.

MAX: Nothing?

TITO: Singing. It's like a–life, eh? You gotta relax, take it easy. You get a–tense, you finished.

MAX: I know what you mean. I—I sing myself, a little.

TITO: You?

MAX: Yeah. I—I—I mean, not like you. I wish I could.

TITO: Hey. Done knock youself down. It's no good. To sing, you need a–confidence. You gotta say, "I'm a–the best. I'm a–Max. I sing good."

MAX: I know. I—I—I mean that's the problem. Whenever I sing in front of people, I—I get tense. I tighten up. I can't help it.

TITO: That's it, eh? That's a–me, now. My doctor, he says take a– pills. Phenobarbital. It makes–a you sleep. But I'm–a Merelli. I done take pills.

MAX *(to himself)*: Phenobarbital.

(During the following, MAX picks up SAUNDERS' bottle of pheno- barbital from the table, where MAGGIE left it)

TITO: Hey! I got it. We have a drink. A little wine, eh?

MAX: Hm? No! No, I—I—I don't think that's such a—*(He looks at the bottle of pills)* Well. All right.

TITO: You got a–glasses? I got a good Chianti.

MAX: I—I don't know.

TITO: You gonna join me.

(He heads for the bedroom)

MAX: Right. Okay. One glass!

(MAX *disappears into the kitchenette as* TITO *enters the bedroom.* MARIA *is lying on the bed, on her stomach, still reading* Vogue)

TITO: *Ciao.*

MARIA: *Ciao.*

(She ignores him. TITO *looks at her)*

TITO: Eh. *Bellezza.* I'm a–sorry. Okay?

MARIA: Phh.

TITO: I get a–tense. It's too much. It's a–my fault.

MARIA: Yeah.

TITO: Hey. Listen. We take a vacation. Soon. *(He sits on the bed)* Greece, eh? We get a boat. We sail a–the islands. Sleep all day. On the sand. *(He's rubbing her backside)* Just a–two, eh. Like a– the old days. Clams. Big lobster. Suck a–the claws.

MARIA *(warming considerably):* Tito . . .

TITO: *Bellezza.*

(They get intimate. She's kissing his neck)

MARIA: Close a–door.

TITO: Huh?

MARIA: Close a–door.

TITO: Now?

MARIA: Close.

TITO: Maria. I got a stomach. No joke.

MARIA: I make a–you better. Fix you up.

TITO: No. Hey. Not now, okay? I—I can't do it!

(She stops, angry)

MARIA: Pig!

TITO: Maria!

MARIA: You got a girl.

TITO: I got nobody.

MARIA: You got a girl! So done lie!

TITO: Maria—

MARIA: Three weeks—nothing! Not once, eh?

TITO: I'm sorry. I get a–tense. I—I got a stomach!

MARIA: I wanna be a nun, I'll join a–the church! At least sometimes I have a–some fun. I sing a–hymns. Pluck a–chickens!

TITO: She's crazy. My wife, she's a–crazy.

MARIA: Oh sure, I'm a–crazy. I hate a–trains, I'm a–crazy. I hate hotels. I'm a–crazy. I got a–empty bed, and I'm a–crazy!

TITO: Maria, I'm a sick a–man!

MARIA: SO TAKE A–YOU PILLS!

TITO *(angry):* Fine. Okay. I take a–pills! *(He goes to the vanity case and takes out his bottle of pills)* You wanna pills, I take a–pills. Look! Hey! Two pills. No. *Four* pills!

MARIA: Two!

TITO: Four!!

MARIA: Oh!

TITO: Okay? Happy?

(He puts the bottle on the bedside table)

MARIA: Phh!

TITO: I take a–pills, I got a happy wife. Happy marriage!

(He pulls a bottle of Chianti from the vanity case)

MARIA: Now you gonna be sick.

TITO: So what? My girl in the closet, she's not gonna care.

MARIA: Pig!

TITO: SHUT UP!

MARIA: SHUT UP A–YOUSELF!

(MARIA slams into the bathroom. TITO slams into the sitting room)

TITO: Max!

(He paces, upset. MAX enters from the kitchenette with two glasses)

MAX: Are you all right?

TITO: I'm a–peachy. Just a–fine. I done relax, I'm gonna blow up! Open!

(He hands MAX the bottle)

MAX *(taking it):* Uh, s–sorry. Corkscrew?

TITO: Eh? Oh yeah. Corkascrew. Sure. I'm a–stupid!

(TITO enters the bedroom, grabs the vanity case and sits on the bed. As he looks for the corkscrew, MAX unscrews the top from the bottle of phenobarbital and pours several pills into one of the

glasses. He thinks for a moment, then pours more pills. Beat. Then adds a few more for good measure. By this time, TITO *has found the corkscrew. He slams back into the sitting room as* MAX *pockets the bottle of pills.* TITO *grabs the Chianti and starts opening it)*

TITO: Jealousy, eh? That's all I get is a–jealousy. Back a–stage. Girls, they come a–see me. Nice girls. They wanna my auto- graph. That's it. They say, "Hello, Tito. We love a–you, Tito." Maria, she goes a–nuts.

MAX: I'll pour.

(MAX *takes the bottle, fills* TITO*'s glass and hands it to him. Then he puts his finger into* TITO*'s glass and stirs.* TITO *watches, star- tled, then bemused. He looks at* MAX. MAX *removes his finger and acts as if nothing's wrong. Beat)*

TITO: Hey. You join me.

MAX: Gee, I—I—I don't really—

TITO: Drink!

MAX: Right. *(He pours some wine into his own glass and raises it)* Well. Down the hatch.

(TITO *pauses. Then ceremoniously, proud to know the local ritual, he puts his finger into* MAX*'s glass and stirs.* MAX *looks sick)*

TITO: *Salut.*

(TITO *drains his glass as* MAX *watches. For a moment,* TITO *senses something strange; then he sighs with pleasure at the effect of the wine.* MAX *is clearly relieved)*

MAX: I think you're going to feel a lot better now.

TITO: I hope so, eh? 'Cause worse would be impossible.

(TITO *sits down heavily)*

MAX: You—you might even take a nap. Who knows.

TITO: Sure. Who knows. *(He picks up the bottle and starts pouring himself more wine)* Miracles happen, eh?

MAX *(trying to stop him):* Mr. Merelli, I—I—I—

TITO: Tito! You call me Tito. 'Cause I like you.

MAX: Uh . . . right. Tito. *(It's too late. The wine is poured.* MAX *takes the bottle)* Good year.

(He puts the bottle down as far from TITO *as possible)*

TITO: *Salut.*

(As TITO *drinks, the bathroom door swings open and* MARIA *stalks into the bedroom)*

MARIA *(to herself):* No more! That's it! I'm a–finished with that man!

(During the following, she finds a pen and a piece of paper in her vanity case, then sits on the bed and starts to write her farewell note to TITO*)*

TITO *(relaxing):* Hey. Max. Sing a–me something.

MAX: Huh?

TITO: You sing, I listen. Maybe I help, eh? Make a–pointer.

MAX: Gee, that's awfully—Now?

TITO: Sure. Why not? Free lesson.

MAX: Well, I—I—I suppose . . .

TITO: Come on. Let's hear. Stand up!

MAX *(standing):* Right. Is there, uh, anything special?

TITO: Pick a–you favorite. Go.

MAX: Right. *(He is nervous and embarrassed. He clears his throat, then gropes for the right pitch)* Ahem . . . Okay . . . *(Without much confidence, he starts to sing. He's chosen the tenor line of the duet "Dio, che nell'alma infondere," from Act II, Scene 1 of Verdi's* Don Carlo. *He sings without accompaniment and not very well)*
Dio, che nell'alma infondere
amor volesti e speme—

TITO: Stop! (MAX *stops)* Okay. You're a–tight, eh? Tense. Is no good. You gotta relax. Be you.

MAX: I—I—I'm trying. I—

TITO: Okay, now shake a–youself.

MAX: Huh?

TITO: Shake! Like this. *(Standing by now, he shakes his body, arms flailing in a singer's exercise)* Come on! *(Tentatively,* MAX *imitates him)* Move! (MAX *lets loose. They both move around the room, arms flailing)* Good. Okay. Now the throat. It's a–tight. It's gotta be loose. Like this. *(He rolls his head in a circle, around his shoulders, simultaneously singing a note)* Ahhh . . .

MAX *(joining):* Ahhh . . .

(THEY continue for a few seconds, then stop. MAX *holds his forehead to stop the dizziness)*

TITO: Now . . . together.

(They sing "ah," roll their heads and move around the room, arms flailing. After a few seconds, TITO *stops and watches* MAX, *who eventually notices that he's doing it alone. He straightens up)*

TITO: Now—a trick, eh? You gotta hear the music. Before you sing. You gotta hear everything. The orchestra, the chorus—

MAX *(enthusiastic):* I—I know what you mean!

TITO: Everything! It's in a–you heart!

MAX: Right!

TITO: Okay. Shh! Listen!

(Silence. Then four notes, pizzicato, from the orchestra—which is now in their heads. A fifth note swells and they begin the duet)

MAX AND TITO *(singing, with full orchestra):*
Dio, che nell'alma infondere
amor volesti e speme,
desio nel cor accendere
tu sei di liberta;
desio accendere, accender nel cor
tu sei di liberta.
Giuriamo insiem di vivere
e di morire insieme.
In terra, in ciel
congiungere ci puo,
ci puo la tua bonta.
Ah! Dio che nell'alma, [etc.]

(Their duet gets progressively more confident and dramatic. Meanwhile, MARIA stands, having finished her note. She scans it with tears in her eyes, folds it in half and props it on the bed, on top of the pillow. Note: *The paper should be distinctive and easy to recognize—lavender, perhaps. She picks up her vanity case, heads for the door to the corridor and opens it. She stops. She forgot something—her fur stole. She goes to the closet, opens it and MAGGIE falls out, having fallen asleep inside, against the door. The following is heard over the singing, as it occurs during the quiet second verse)*

MAGGIE: How do you do. I realize this may look a little strange, but I can explain it—(MARIA *stifles a growl of anger; then reaches into the closet, takes the stole and turns away)* You see, I admire your husband and I just wanted his autograph so I thought, well, why not hide in the closet. *(Stole in one hand, vanity case in the other,* MARIA *stalks out)* Wait! You don't understand! I don't even know him!

(MAGGIE runs out after MARIA, closing the door behind her. Meanwhile, TITO and MAX finish their duet)

TITO AND MAX *(singing):*
Vivremo insiem, morremo insiem!
Grido estremo sara:
Liberta!

TITO: Haha!

MAX: Haha!

TITO: That's a–wonderful! That's a–beautiful! You sing a–beautiful!

MAX *(overlapping):* I—I—I see what you mean! I felt so good! I mean, I—I felt relaxed!

TITO: Ohh! That was work, eh? Hoo!

MAX: It was great!

(They calm down)

TITO: Hey. Guess what. I think I'm a–tired.

MAX: Oh. I—I'm sorry. I—

TITO: No! That's a–good. I'm gonna sleep.

MAX: Oh. Oh good! That—that's great.

TITO *(yawning):* Yahh! Hoo. *(He stands up unsteadily)* Max. You wake a–me, eh? Six–thirty.

MAX: Right. Sure. I promise. (TITO *heads for the bedroom)* Uh . . . Tito, thanks, for the lesson.

TITO: Hey. You sing good. No joke. You got real promise.

MAX: Thanks.

TITO: We talk a–more, later. Okay?

MAX: Sure. And if you need anything, just holler.

(TITO *goes into the bedroom and closes the door.* MAX, *who feels wonderful, sits and daydreams. He sips his Chianti.* TITO *is exhausted now—drugged, in fact. He realizes that* MARIA *isn't there. He looks around. He calls toward the bathroom)*

TITO: Maria! Hey. I'm gonna sleep. Okay? *(No answer)* Maria. I'm gonna sleep . . . *(He knocks)* Okay? *(No answer. He shrugs, and with a groan, stretches out on the bed until he comes nose-to-nose with* MARIA's *note. He picks it up and reads it. Pause. A scream)* NOOOO!!! (MAX *bounds out of his chair and runs to the bedroom)* No! No! No! *(He drops the note on the bedside table)*

MAX *(flying into the bedroom):* What happened?!

TITO: Impossible!

MAX: What?!

TITO: No!!

MAX: WHAT HAPPENED?!!

TITO: She's a–gone! Maria!

MAX: Gone where?

TITO *(shaking* MAX): Gone! Gone! She's a–gone!

MAX: Tito!!!

TITO *(releasing him):* She's a–left me! For good!

MAX: Are you sure?

TITO: SHE'S A–GONE!

MAX: Now—now—now wait a second. Maybe she went downstairs. For—for a magazine.

TITO: Look! Look!! No case! *(He flings open the closet door)* No fur!

MAX: I guess she's gone.

TITO: MARIA!! NO! NO! NO!

MAX: TITO! CALM DOWN!

TITO *(sitting):* Max . . . Max . . .

MAX: Now listen! We—we—we can look for her. We'll look in the lobby—

TITO: It's a–my fault. I give her trouble. She's not a–happy. *(Crying)* Me! I make her unhappy!

MAX: Tito . . .

TITO: She hates a–me. I wanna kill myself.

MAX: She'll come back. You'll see.

TITO: I'm gonna kill myself!

(He jumps up and runs into the sitting room)

MAX: Stop!

(MAX runs after him. TITO looks wildly around the room for his instrument of destruction. He picks up the Chianti bottle and tries to stab himself with it. No good. He tosses it away and MAX catches it, still chasing him)

TITO: I'm gonna kill myself!! I live a–no more!!

MAX: Calm down!

TITO: No more!

MAX: Hey, please!

TITO: She hates a–me! I hate a–myself!

(TITO rushes into the kitchenette)

MAX: No, Tito!

(MAX *follows him. Noise of a struggle*)

MAX *(offstage):* Tito, stop it!

TITO *(offstage):* Get away!

MAX *(offstage):* Don't! Hey!

(A crash—a drawer of cutlery hitting the floor. A second later TITO *runs out, followed by* MAX. TITO *is holding a fork)*

MAX: Tito!

TITO: I'm gonna kill myself!!!

MAX: *Put down that fork!!!*

TITO: She hates a–me! It's all over!

MAX: Tito! This is not an opera! Please! Put it down!

*(*TITO *drops the fork and collapses onto the sofa, exhausted)*

TITO: Oh, Max! *Max!*

MAX: It's all right. You'll be fine.

TITO: She's a–gone.

MAX: It's not your fault.

TITO: Oh, Maria. Maria . . .

MAX: She'll come back. You'll see. (TITO *picks up the Chianti bottle and starts to drink)* Hey! Hey, no! Stop! *(He takes the bottle)* Come on. Get up. Let's get you to bed.

TITO: I can't.

MAX: LET'S GO!

(MAX *pulls* TITO *to his feet, and, holding him up, leads him to the bedroom*)

TITO: Max, she hates a–me.

MAX: Nooo. She loves you. She'll come back.

TITO: I wanna kill myself.

MAX: Into bed. Come on.

(*He lays* TITO *down on the bed. Throughout the following,* TITO *becomes increasingly limp and dizzy. His speech slurs with exhaustion*)

TITO: Bed . . .

MAX: You'll get a good sleep. You'll feel a lot better. I promise.

TITO: Sleep . . .

MAX: We'll take off your shoes.

(*He pulls* TITO's *shoes off. It's a struggle*)

TITO: Shoes . . .

MAX: Uuuh! There. I'll bet that feels good. Huh? Now close your eyes . . . I'll be right inside . . .

TITO: Max!

MAX: Huh?

TITO: Max. Done leave me! Stay! Please!

MAX: Okay. Right. I'm here.

TITO (*faintly*): Stay . . .

MAX: I—I—I'm right here. Here I am. See? Okay?

TITO *(fainter):* Sleep . . .

MAX: Shhh. That's right. A good sleep . . . Off you go . . .

(Pause. All is quiet. MAX *sits on the edge of the bed)*

TITO: Max!

MAX *(falling off the bed):* I'm right here!

TITO: Max . . . sing . . .

MAX *(getting back on the bed):* Huh?

TITO: Maria. She sings a–me. I sleep . . .

MAX: Oh. I see.

TITO *(faint):* Sing . . .

MAX: Right. *(He clears his throat)* Is there, uh . . . anything special?

TITO: Sing!

MAX: Sing.

*(*MAX *tries feebly to get the pitch, as before. Then he remembers the lesson and shuts his eyes to conjure up the orchestra. A french horn sounds the pitch in* MAX's *head. He looks up and smiles. Then softly he begins to sing the tenor line from the* Don Carlo *duet)*

MAX *(singing):*
Dio, che nell'alma infondere
amor volesti e speme,
desio nel cor accendere [etc.]

(As TITO *falls asleep, he reaches for* MAX's *hand and holds it.* MAX *pats* TITO's *hand and continues singing. The lights fade as the sound of the orchestra takes over the musical theme)*

Scene 2

Four hours later. About 6:30 p.m. MAX *and* TITO *are asleep.* MAX *is in the sitting room on the sofa.* TITO *is stretched out on the bed, under the covers. As the music fades the telephone starts ringing.* MAX *wakes up, disoriented. He answers the phone.*

MAX: Hello?

BELLHOP *(singing through the phone):*
Largo al factotum
della citta, largo!
La ran la, la ran la,
la ran la, la!

MAX: Thank you—

BELLHOP *(through the phone):* It's six–thirty! This is your wake-up call!

MAX *(into the phone):* Thanks . . . Hm? . . . No. He's sleeping . . . No, you can't meet him . . . Not now! N—(MAX *sighs)* Look. All right. If you bring up some coffee, you can meet him for a second . . . I promise!

BELLHOP *(through the phone):* Yahoooo!

(There's a knock at the sitting room/corridor door)

MAX *(hanging up the phone):* Coming! (MAX *goes to the door and opens it. It's* DIANA. *She's in her mid–thirties. Beautiful and very sexy)* Diana.

DIANA: Hi, Max. *(She strolls in, looks around)* Nice place.

MAX: Yeah. Well, you know. Tito Merelli.

DIANA: Of course.

(She wanders into the room, in no hurry)

MAX: How was rehearsal?

DIANA: Not too bad. Considering I had to sing the duets by myself.

MAX: Yeah, I'm—I'm sorry about that. He'll be there tonight, though. No problem.

DIANA: It might work better that way.

(MAX *looks at his watch)*

MAX: Diana . . . is there, uh, anything I can do for you?

DIANA: I just thought I'd stop by and say hello. I thought it might be preferable to meeting him onstage.

MAX: Gee, that's—that's nice of you, but the thing is, he's uh, he's sleeping right now. He's taking a nap.

DIANA *(sitting):* I can wait. There's no hurry.

MAX: Yeah, well—actually, I—I thought it might be better if I got him to the theatre first and then he could meet everybody at the same time. I mean, I've got to wake him, and he has to get ready and—and he might want some time alone. If you see what I mean.

DIANA: Do you know what he could do for me, Max? One call from Tito Merelli and I'd be at the Met in two days.

MAX: Yeah—

DIANA: So you see, Max, it's very important to me that I get to know him. Spend a little time with him. Do you understand?

MAX: Yeah, I do. I really do. Except right now, the thing is just to get him there and—and then later, you'll have plenty of time. I mean he'll—he'll be here tomorrow. Right? Okay.

(Pause)

DIANA: You're very cute, Max. Has anyone ever told you that before?

MAX: Sure. My—my mother. My Aunt Harriet.

DIANA: Anyone single?

MAX: My Uncle Bud.

DIANA: You aren't going to let me see him, are you, Max?

MAX: Later. I promise. I'll—I'll arrange it so you have lots of time with him. Alone. Okay? I promise.

DIANA: Will you give him a message for me?

MAX: Sure. Anything.

DIANA: Tell him this.

(She puts her hand behind MAX's neck and kisses him on the lips. It's a very long kiss. He doesn't know what to do with his arms. She breaks it off)

MAX: YAHH!! I'll tell him. Of course he might misunderstand.

DIANA: See you later, Max.

(She picks up her purse and exits, closing the door. MAX sighs with relief)

MAX *(he looks at his watch):* Oh jeez. *(He hurries to the connecting door and knocks)* Tito. It's time to get up. *(He opens the door and switches on the bedroom light)* Sorry. (MAX *leaves the door open and turns back into the sitting room. During the following, he picks up the Chianti bottle and glasses and heads for the kitchenette.* TITO *continues sleeping)* I ordered some coffee, but if you want anything else, I can call downstairs. (MAX *goes into the kitchenette, then comes out again a moment later, having disposed of the bottle and glasses)* Are you hungry? Tito? *(No answer.* MAX *goes to the connecting door, looks in the bedroom and sees that* TITO *is still asleep)* Tito. It's time to get up. You'll be late. (MAX *enters the bedroom and walks to the bed. He shakes* TITO) Hey, come on. I hate to wake you, but it's quarter to seven. *(No response)* Tito . . . Let's go! *(He pulls* TITO *up by the arms and releases him.* TITO *flops back on the bed)* What's the matter? Tito, wake up! *(He shakes him harder)* Tito! *(No response.* MAX *straightens up and stares at* TITO, *suddenly afraid. Something is definitely wrong. He then notices a folded note on the bedside table—*MARIA*'s note, which happens to be next to* TITO*'s bottle of pills. He hesitates, then picks up the note and reads it. Reading)* "By the time you get this, I'll be gone forever." (MAX *stiffens, looks at* TITO, *then back at the note)* "After what has happened, it's just not worth to me the pain and unhappiness of staying around any more. The fun is gone and now, so am I. *Ciao.*" *(He stares at the note, horrified. He then sees the bottle of pills and picks it up. It's empty)* Tito! Wake up! *(He shakes him violently)* Tito, for God's sake! *(A knock at the sitting room/corridor door.* MAX *doesn't hear it and continues shaking* TITO) Tito, can you hear me? Tito! Please! Tito!

SAUNDERS *(offstage):* Max?

MAX *(shaking him again):* Tito, wake up! Please wake up! *Come on! (Suddenly,* MAX *stops shaking him. He realizes that it's no use.* TITO *is gone.* MAX *is white as a sheet)* Oh my God.

SAUNDERS *(offstage, knocking):* Open the door, Max!

MAX *(calling):* C–coming! One second! (MAX *looks at* TITO *sadly. He's lost a friend)* Tito. I'm so sorry.

SAUNDERS *(offstage, still knocking):* Max! Open the door!

(MAX *turns away and walks into the sitting room, closing the connecting door behind him. He's in a daze, but makes it to the corridor door and opens it.* SAUNDERS *enters, in white tie for the evening's festivities)*

SAUNDERS: Well thank you, Max. I hope that wasn't too much trouble. *(No response)* And how is Il Stupendo? Has he recovered yet?

MAX: Recovered?

SAUNDERS: You said on the telephone he was upset. His wife . . . ?

MAX: Oh. Right.

SAUNDERS: Which frankly didn't surprise me at all the way they carried on. I was fully expecting one of them to pull a knife. *(No response)* Is he feeling better? . . . Max?

MAX: Hm?

SAUNDERS: Is he feeling better?

MAX: Sir . . . he's dead.

(Pause)

SAUNDERS: Well I'm not surprised. It must really take it out of you having your wife just walk out the door.

MAX: Sir—

SAUNDERS: Of course it doesn't have to be the best performance he ever gave. Just get him on stage at this point—

MAX: *Sir.*

SAUNDERS: Max?

MAX: He's dead. I mean he . . . he's dead. He killed himself.

(Long pause)

SAUNDERS: Who?

MAX: Tito.

(Pause)

SAUNDERS: Merelli?

MAX *(nodding, he's choked up)*: He's in the bedroom.

(SAUNDERS *eyes* MAX. *Then walks to the connecting door*)

SAUNDERS: Is this a joke?

MAX *(a sob):* No.

(SAUNDERS *opens the door and steps inside.* MAX *follows him to the door.* SAUNDERS *looks at* TITO. *He walks to the bed and pauses. He shakes* TITO's *shoulder. No response. Gingerly, he opens one of* TITO's *eyelids. Nothing. Pause*)

SAUNDERS: Jesus Christ.

MAX: I know.

SAUNDERS: What happened?!

MAX: He—he got upset. About his wife. He took the whole bottle.

SAUNDERS: Jesus Christ!

MAX: He left a note—

(SAUNDERS *snatches the note from* MAX. *He pores over it, as* MAX *continues*)

MAX: I—I—I knew he was upset—he got so excited. I—I mean he grabbed a fork and said he'd kill himself, but then he—he calmed down and he just—just wanted to rest.

SAUNDERS *(squinting at the note):* "The *fur* is gone"?

MAX *(looking):* "Fun." "The fun is gone and now, so am I."

SAUNDERS: Oh my God.

MAX: I—I thought he was exaggerating.

SAUNDERS: They'll crucify me.

MAX: It's not your fault.

SAUNDERS: They'll want their money back! *(Pause)* Italian bastard. I knew he'd get me. *(To* TITO*)* Are you satisfied?! HUH?!

MAX: Sir—

SAUNDERS *(climbing onto the bed and shaking* TITO *violently in a rage):* ARE YOU PROUD OF YOURSELF??!! FEEL BETTER NOW??!! *AHHHHHHH!!!*

MAX *(trying to pull* SAUNDERS *off):* SIR, CALM DOWN!!

(Finally, after several more seconds, SAUNDERS *stops)*

SAUNDERS: Why me? He could have waited until tomorrow. He could have jumped out of the window after breakfast.

MAX: We sang a duet together. I mean I—I really liked him.

*(*SAUNDERS *climbs off the bed)*

SAUNDERS *(bitter):* Well, I guess that wraps it up. End of the road. Arriverderci. *(Suddenly he attacks the body again)* AHHHH!!!

MAX: SIR!!

*(*SAUNDERS *stops. Stands up. Then kicks the bed.* MAX *covers* TITO, *head and all, with the blan   .* SAUNDERS *walks into the sitting room, and* MAX *follows him)*

SAUNDERS: I'll have to make an announcement, of course. A few brief words, nothing elaborate. Ladies and gentlemen—Mr. Tito Merelli killed himself this afternoon, thereby depriving many of us . . . of a great pleasure. It was universally acknowledged that he sang like an angel, but apparently he wanted to prove it. In short, our star for the evening has departed this world in a final gesture of selfishness and deceit unrivalled in the history of comic opera!

MAX: I think maybe I should make the announcement.

*(*SAUNDERS *runs for the connecting door to get at* TITO *again, but* MAX *grabs him)*

SAUNDERS: Ahhhhhhhhhh!

MAX: We—we could still do the performance. I think we should.

SAUNDERS: Oh oh oh absolutely. We can prop him up and play a record. Add a few lines about how he was wounded in the Battle of Cyprus, then carry him around the stage on a stretcher!

MAX: I—I—I mean the understudy.

SAUNDERS: The understudy. Of course! My God, you've solved the whole problem! Skip the announcement, stick a note in the program, "The role of Otello will be sung by Albert Rupp." And then if there is anyone still in the audience when he takes his bow, they can stone him to death! The ultimate operatic experience! One thundering orgasm of insane violence! Make *Salome* look like *The Merry Widow!*

MAX: Sir, I think you ought to calm down.

SAUNDERS: Right! Good point! We don't want two dead bodies around here. Just think of the smell. Put everybody at the Gala Buffet right off their shrimp!

MAX: Sir! Let's just—just sit down for a minute. Okay? Sir? (SAUNDERS *is dazed. Numb. Slowly he sits.* MAX *sits next to him. Pause)* These things happen, sir.

SAUNDERS *(a last lunge;* MAX *grabs him):* AHH!

MAX: It's not your fault. It was just—unlucky, that's all. I mean everybody'll understand.

SAUNDERS: Yes. Of course they will. And then they'll fire me. Ungrateful cruds.

(Pause. The rage is over. Black despair. After several seconds, however, SAUNDERS *smiles. Then he chuckles. More chuckles. Then he breaks into laughter; genuine, if slightly hysterical)*

MAX: What's so funny? . . . Sir? . . .

SAUNDERS: Ohhh! . . . I was just thinking. They probably wouldn't know the difference. Albert Rupp. Black his face. Huge wig, lots of padding. If we didn't tell the audience, they'd think he was Tito Merelli.

MAX: Think so? *(He thinks about it. Then chuckles)* I think you're right. *(He starts to laugh, in spite of himself—which sets off* SAUNDERS *again)* They . . . they probably wouldn't know—

SAUNDERS: They'd give him a standing ovation!

MAX: Bring down the house! *(They both laugh uproariously, out of control. They can't stop. Finally)* Ohhh . . .

SAUNDERS: Ohhh . . .

MAX: It wouldn't work.

SAUNDERS: I know.

MAX: I mean the company would know it was him—

SAUNDERS: Of course.

MAX: And the story would leak out—

SAUNDERS: And then the audience would hang me. Yes, I realize that.

MAX: If he wasn't in the company, I bet it would work.

SAUNDERS: But he is.

MAX: Yeah. Too bad.

(Long pause. Slowly, a light dawns in SAUNDERS' *brain. He rolls it over in his mind, then turns his head and looks at* MAX. MAX *sees him and smiles amiably. He doesn't realize what* SAUNDERS *is thinking. Then he sees the stony, maniacal look in* SAUNDERS' *eyes and suddenly* MAX *looks nervous)*

SAUNDERS *(quietly):* Max.

MAX: Forget it. It wouldn't work. They'd spot me in ten seconds.

SAUNDERS: No they wouldn't.

MAX: Hey, stop it. The answer's no.

SAUNDERS: Max . . .

MAX: You're out of your mind. I don't even look like him.

SAUNDERS: Black face. Lots of hair . . .

MAX: Hey. We were joking. This is life. It's called reality. Remember that?

SAUNDERS: You could do it, Max. I know you could.

MAX *(starting to panic):* Hey. Look. Just—just one second, okay? I don't speak Italian. I—I—I—I—I—I hardly speak English.

SAUNDERS: You wouldn't have to speak Italian. Just sing it.

MAX: Look—look—just—just—okay? They'd know. They would know. It's me. Max.

SAUNDERS: No they wouldn't! That's the point! They've never seen him before. They're expecting *him,* not *you.*

MAX: Yeah, but—but—but—but . . .

SAUNDERS: They want to see him, Max. They want to say they've seen him.

MAX: But it's an opera! Four acts!

SAUNDERS: You know the part. You admitted it.

MAX: I can hum it! In the bathtub!

(The phone rings)

SAUNDERS: You know every single note, I know you do—

MAX: Wrong! There's a few at the end, I—I get mixed up—

SAUNDERS: Aha! *(Into the phone)* Yes?

MAX *(pacing):* You're out of your mind!

SAUNDERS *(into the phone):* Yes, Julia.

MAX: I mean, you're crazy! Okay? You're nuts!

SAUNDERS *(into the phone; he can't hear):* What? *(To* MAX*)* Be quiet.

MAX: They could arrest me! It's called impersonation. Big crime—

SAUNDERS *(into the phone):* No, Tito is much better. He's fine.

MAX: No, he isn't. He's dead. He's not fine. Fine is living!

SAUNDERS *(into the phone):* No! Now, Julia, just listen. Don't come up . . . No. Just stay *downstairs.* Well, frankly, he's still a bit upset about his wife and I think it's better if we meet you backstage.

MAX: That's better. That is better. Because he's dead!

SAUNDERS *(into the phone):* Yes, just Max . . . Right. Fine. See you there. *(He hangs up)*

MAX: That was a mistake.

SAUNDERS: Max . . .

MAX: No.

SAUNDERS: I'm begging you, Max. I'm on my knees. *(He is)*

MAX: No!

SAUNDERS: Look at me! Max. You can do it, believe me!

MAX: I can't!

SAUNDERS: A thousand people! They're getting dressed now. They've got tickets at fifty dollars each, Max. That's fifty thousand dollars!

MAX: Sir—

SAUNDERS: My whole career! My life, Max. My children. It's all in your hands.

(SAUNDERS *grabs* MAX *around the knees and sobs. He looks up. No reaction. He sobs harder, sinking to* MAX's *ankles*)

MAX: Ohhhh, *crap!*

SAUNDERS: I'll never forget this, Max.

MAX: I bet.

(SAUNDERS *jumps to his feet and races into the bedroom.* MAX, *now speechless with fear, follows him. During the following,* SAUNDERS *takes one of the suitcases from the closet and puts it on the bed next to* TITO)

SAUNDERS: I have it all figured out. It's simple. You change here, make–up, the works. Then we drive to the theatre just in time and suddenly, bang, you're onstage.

MAX: Oh God.

SAUNDERS: Between the acts, you'll stay in your dressing room. Locked up. Then, after it's over, it's straight to the car, drive back and we're finished.

MAX: What about, uh . . . *(He nods at* TITO)

SAUNDERS: No problem. Tomorrow morning, we break the news. He took the pills *after* the performance and passed away quietly during the night. This is it. *(The costume.* SAUNDERS *rummages through the suitcase)* Costume . . . make–up . . . wig . . . *(A knock at the sitting room/corridor door. They both freeze)* Who's that?

MAX: How should I know?!

SAUNDERS: I'll take care of it. You just change, and make it quick.

(He hands MAX *the suitcase and heads for the sitting room)*

MAX: Sir?

SAUNDERS *(stopping):* Yes, Max?

MAX: Wish me luck.

SAUNDERS: We don't need luck, Max.

MAX: Thanks.

(MAX *enters the bathroom.* SAUNDERS *leaves the bedroom and closes the door)*

SAUNDERS: We need a miracle. *(He walks to the sitting room/ corridor door)* Who is it?

JULIA *(offstage):* It's me, Henry. Open the door.

SAUNDERS: Julia! I told you not to come up!

JULIA *(offstage):* Open the door, Henry! (SAUNDERS *opens the door.* JULIA *enters. She's about sixty and wears a silver dress covered in sequins. She strikes a pose)* How do I look? The truth.

SAUNDERS: Like the Chrysler Building.

JULIA: I knew you'd like it. *(She sweeps in and twirls around)* It's straight from Paris. Haute couture. I feel like one of those fancy French tarts.

SAUNDERS: Julia, for God's sake—

JULIA: Now, don't be cross, Henry. I couldn't bear waiting backstage anymore. Not with those shrimp. I could hardly breathe. Besides, I thought I might cheer him up. The woman's touch. Suddenly before he knows it he'll feel vital again. Totally alive.

SAUNDERS: No, I don't think so.

JULIA: You know what this reminds me of? That opera, the one with the snow falling, and the violins and everybody's hungry all the time.

SAUNDERS: Julia, please! Just *listen!*

JULIA: I'm listening, Henry.

SAUNDERS: I want you to go to the theatre. Now. All right? As a favor to me.

JULIA: Oh, Henry. You know how I feel about you.

SAUNDERS *(moving towards the door):* Good. Off you go—

JULIA: But it's just so silly. I'm here already.

SAUNDERS: But you won't be soon. You'll be at the theatre.

JULIA *(logically):* Not if I'm here. I can't be in two places.

SAUNDERS: You won't be in two places. You won't be here.

JULIA: Why not?

SAUNDERS: Because you'll be there.

JULIA: But why bother? I'm already here—

SAUNDERS: Julia, please—! *(A knock at the door)* Now what?!

JULIA *(sitting):* I think it's the door.

(SAUNDERS *stops halfway to the door, returns to just behind* JULIA *and raises his arm as though he's going to slug her over the head, backhanded. He controls himself and returns to the door)*

SAUNDERS *(at the door):* Who is it?!

BELLHOP *(offstage):* Room service. Coffee for two.

SAUNDERS: We didn't order any coffee.

BELLHOP *(offstage): You did so! Ask Max!*

SAUNDERS: Well, it's cancelled!

JULIA *(going to the door):* Oh stop it, Henry. You can't just let him stand there.

SAUNDERS: Don't—!

(She opens the door. The BELLHOP *enters, holding a tray with a coffee service on it. He also has a camera hanging around his neck. He leaves the door open)*

BELLHOP: Thank you, madam.

JULIA: On the table, please.

SAUNDERS: And then get out.

JULIA: He's only doing his job, Henry.

SAUNDERS: Well, he can do it somewhere else.

BELLHOP: Shall I pour, madam?

JULIA: Thank you, that would be very nice.

SAUNDERS: Julia, I want you out of here!

BELLHOP: He's not very friendly, is he?

SAUNDERS: Julia, please! You promised!

JULIA: I wonder what's keeping Mr. Merelli?

BELLHOP: Is he getting dressed?

JULIA: Apparently.

BELLHOP *(going to the connecting door):* Perhaps he needs some help with his buttons. You know these opera stars, they're helpless—

SAUNDERS: STOP! *(The* BELLHOP *stops, his hand on the doorknob)* Take one step into that room and I will *kill* you.

BELLHOP: Fair enough. I'll wait out here.

SAUNDERS: You're not waiting anyplace, you're getting out!

BELLHOP: Fine. . . . As soon as I meet him. *(He sits)*

SAUNDERS: You're not meeting him.

BELLHOP: Max promised. That's why I brought the coffee. I'm a bellhop, not a waiter.

SAUNDERS: Listen, you—!!

(In a burst of anger, SAUNDERS *grabs the* BELLHOP *by his shirtfront and hoists him to his feet. Simultaneously* MAGGIE *appears at the sitting room/corridor door dressed for the evening. She carries a single red rose)*

JULIA: Henry!

BELLHOP: Help!

MAGGIE *(rushing in):* Daddy!

BELLHOP: Help!

MAGGIE: What are you doing?

SAUNDERS *(to the* BELLHOP*):* Are you getting out?

BELLHOP: I'm getting wrinkled.

MAGGIE: Daddy, stop it! What's the matter?

*(*SAUNDERS *drops the* BELLHOP*)*

BELLHOP *(smoothing himself out):* We had a slight misunderstanding. Then he went insane.

SAUNDERS *(to MAGGIE):* What the hell are you doing here?

MAGGIE: I came to see Mr. Merelli. To—to wish him luck.

SAUNDERS: Well, you're not going to, so get out!

MAGGIE: Daddy, what's the matter with you? Has something happened?

SAUNDERS *(after a slight pause):* No.

JULIA: He's been under a lot of strain lately. Haven't you, Henry?

SAUNDERS: No!

BELLHOP: Yes, you have, Henry. I can tell.

SAUNDERS: Get him out of here. I'm warning you.

MAGGIE *(to the BELLHOP):* This isn't like him at all.

BELLHOP: Oh yes it is.

SAUNDERS: Get out!! Now!!

BELLHOP: All right!! *(With dignity)* I will be happy to leave—

JULIA *(to SAUNDERS):* There.

BELLHOP: As soon as I get one picture.

SAUNDERS: Give me the camera.

BELLHOP: No.

SAUNDERS *(advancing):* Hand it over, you little twit!

BELLHOP *(retreating):* Stay away from me!

MAGGIE: Daddy!

JULIA: Henry!

(SAUNDERS *chases the* BELLHOP *around the sofa, with* MAGGIE *and* JULIA *chasing* SAUNDERS)

BELLHOP: *Hold it!*

(The BELLHOP *snaps a picture of the other three, who pose momentarily without realizing it. Then, immediately the chase resumes)*

SAUNDERS: I want the camera!

(As the chase continues in the sitting room, the bathroom door opens and MAX *emerges, dressed head to foot as Otello in colorful doublet, hose, boots and cape. His face and neck are blackened with make–up and he wears black gloves and a large, black wig. He also wears his glasses. He staggers into the bedroom, visibly quaking. He makes it to the connecting door and puts his ear against it. The action in the sitting room has continued without a break)*

JULIA: Henry!

BELLHOP: Help!

SAUNDERS *(to* MAGGIE*)*: Get the camera! Maggie!

JULIA: Henry, let him take the picture.

BELLHOP: Henry!

SAUNDERS: Gotcha! *(He grabs him)*

BELLHOP: All right! Okay! I give up!

SAUNDERS: Little creep!

*(*MAX *raps sharply on the connecting door. The others freeze and turn to the noise)*

JULIA: It's him!

MAGGIE: He must be ready.

JULIA *(calling):* Mr. Merelli? Is that you?

MAX *(from the bedroom, after a slight pause): Ciao.*

SAUNDERS: Jesus Christ.

JULIA *(calling):* We're all waiting for you.

MAX *(heavy accent):* Please. Send a–me in a–da room, a–Meester Sounders.

JULIA: What a beautiful accent.

MAGGIE *(nudging him):* Daddy . . .

SAUNDERS: I heard him, thank you.

JULIA *(calling):* He'll be right in!

SAUNDERS: Julia. Maggie. I'm asking you for one last time to leave the room.

MAGGIE: But I've got to talk to him!

SAUNDERS: Margaret—

MAGGIE: It's important!

JULIA: Oh, Henry, don't be such a pill. He has to meet us some time.

MAGGIE: Please?

JULIA *(to* MAGGIE): Now don't you worry. You're staying right here. And so am I.

MAX *(from the bedroom):* 'Allo?

JULIA: Henry. Go inside!

SAUNDERS: You're going to regret this, Julia.

JULIA: You always say that and I never do.

MAX: 'Allo?!

SAUNDERS: I'm coming!! *(He goes to the connecting door and turns the knob)* It's me. (MAX *hides behind the door as* SAUNDERS *backs into the bedroom, shielding it from the others. He closes the door—then sees* MAX *and jumps backwards)* Good God!

(JULIA, MAGGIE *and the* BELLHOP *are by this time listening at the door, straining to hear what's happening)*

MAX *(loud)*: I can't do it!!

SAUNDERS *(hissing)*: Keep it down!

MAX *(whispering)*: I can't do it!

SAUNDERS: Max. You look terrific!

MAX: You're crazy!

SAUNDERS: You'll be wonderful!

MAX: No I won't. Believe me.

MAGGIE *(in the sitting room, to* JULIA*)*: What are they saying?

JULIA: I can't hear a thing.

(The BELLHOP, MAGGIE *and* JULIA *disperse from the door)*

SAUNDERS: You'll get a curtain call just for the costume.

MAX: Fine. Then you wear it!

SAUNDERS: Max, we have a bargain. You promised.

MAX: I know. I'm sorry. I'll—I'll—I'll make it up to you. I'll pay you money. Big money—

SAUNDERS: Now just relax! Sit down! You're wound up over nothing.

MAX *(sitting; hysterical):* Nothing . . .

SAUNDERS: Think of it, Max. Your voice, alone, fills the theatre to the second balcony. No one breathes . . .

MAX *(removing his glasses):* Including me. That's the trouble.

SAUNDERS: You can do it, Max.

MAX: I can't.

SAUNDERS: It's your big break. Everything you've ever dreamed about—

MAX: I can't even walk! *(Increasingly panicked)* I—I—I'm shaking all over! I'm losing weight!

SAUNDERS: Max—

MAX: Please!! I'll do anything else! I promise!

SAUNDERS: Max, get a hold of yourself!

MAX *(near tears):* You don't understand! *I can't do it!!* I'm sorry.

(Pause. SAUNDERS *realizes that it's no use. He sighs heavily. He's done all he can)*

SAUNDERS: All right, Max. Go change. I'll make an announcement. I suppose it wouldn't have worked anyway.

*(*SAUNDERS *steels himself, grimly, and leaves the bedroom, closing the door behind him.* MAX *remains where he is and doesn't move)*

JULIA: Well?!

MAGGIE: Where is he?!

BELLHOP: What happened?!

SAUNDERS: Please. I have a short announcement to make. Mr. Merelli has been under a great deal of strain lately. Indeed, as some of you know, today was not one of his better days.

JULIA: Henry!

MAGGIE: What's the matter?!

JULIA: Is he sick?!

SAUNDERS: Mr. Merelli . . . has unexpectedly taken ill.

(Stunned silence)

MAGGIE: Oh no.

SAUNDERS: He will not be singing in this evening's performance.

JULIA: Henry, you must be joking!

SAUNDERS: I'm afraid not.

JULIA *(horrified):* Oh my God! *(She sits)* Henry, do something!

SAUNDERS: There's nothing I can do.

JULIA: Oh my God!

MAGGIE: It's my fault. It's all my fault.

SAUNDERS: Maggie—

MAGGIE: It is!

JULIA: Henry, talk to him! Tell him it's too late to get sick! Say something!

SAUNDERS: I tried, believe me.

(Without warning, MAGGIE *bolts towards the bedroom)*

MAGGIE: Mr. Merelli!

SAUNDERS: Maggie!

(Too late. She swings the door open. MAX *sees* MAGGIE *and bounds to the door. To prevent her from seeing* TITO's *body, he advances into the sitting room, closing the connecting door behind him)*

MAGGIE: Please! I've got to talk to you! (MAX *is speechless. So are the others)* Mr. Merelli, I—I know you've had a bad day, and—and you aren't feeling well. And I'm sure you don't feel like singing tonight, after what happened. But the thing is, everybody's counting on you. I mean, they've all been waiting, for months, and . . . and looking forward to it. And it really won't matter if it isn't your very best, I mean just so it's *you.* And . . . and I know it's asking a lot, but . . . if you could do it—even the first act—we'd all be so grateful. So. . . . Could you? Please?

(MAX *is stunned. He looks at* MAGGIE. *Then at* SAUNDERS. *Then back at* MAGGIE. *Pause)*

MAX *(shrugging, speaking with an accent):* Sure. Why not, eh?

(All hell breaks loose. MAGGIE, JULIA *and the* BELLHOP *surround him, all talking at once. The following three speeches are simultaneous)*

MAGGIE: Oh thank you! Thank you so much! You have no idea how much this means to me. I mean, I know it'll be a strain for you, after what happened—

JULIA: Oh, Mr. Merelli! I cannot tell you what a relief this is to me. And on behalf of the Opera Guild, I want to thank you, from the bottom of my heart, for your courage and—and sacrifice in the face of adversity—

BELLHOP: What a guy. *(Pumping his hand)* Mr. Merelli, my name's Frank, and I've always wanted to meet you since I was this high. And I've got to tell you that everything I've read about you is true. I mean I'm really impressed—

SAUNDERS: HOLD IT!! *(They fall silent)* If we don't leave immediately, he'll miss the curtain.

BELLHOP: Oh my God. I've got to change! I'll see you there! *(He
exits, running)*

SAUNDERS: Julia. Shall we go?

JULIA: Yes of course. I fly on wings of song. *(She exits)*

SAUNDERS: Maggie?

MAGGIE: I'm coming. (SAUNDERS *exits.* MAX *turns away, but* MAG-
GIE *hasn't left yet)* Oh, Mr. Merelli, I've got to talk to you!

MAX: Huh? Hey. We talk later, eh? I, uh, got to prepare myself—

MAGGIE: It's about your wife. I did something terrible!

MAX: Moggie. Pleese. *(Pause)* There are some, few moments
when we done look back and we done look ahead. And for that
a–one moment, we have a–music, we have a–happiness, we
have a–hope. Eh? That's all.

MAGGIE *(handing him the rose she brought with her):* This is for
you.

MAX *(accepting it): Grazie.*

(She extends her hand and they shake. But MAX *doesn't let go. He
turns her hand over and gives her a lingering kiss on the palm. She
stares at him, speechless; looks at her hand; then reels out of the
room, light–headed.* MAX *watches her exit. He's stunned. Long
pause. Then he falls to his knees, sobbing with fear. In the process,
he drops the rose. After a moment, he hears [and we hear] two
voices—his own and* TITO's—*singing the final moments of the*
Don Carlo *duet that they sang in Scene One. The music grows
louder and swells in beauty.* MAX *listens to it; then sees the rose
and picks it up and smells it. His courage grows. He gets to his feet
and stands up straight and tall. As the music continues,* MAX *turns
majestically and walks to the corridor door, arms out, cape billow-
ing behind him. At the threshold, he pauses and turns back. He*

comes to the footlights, acknowledges the thundering applause in his head, throws a kiss to the audience and then turns again and hurries out of the door to his debut.

At this moment—in the bedroom—the covers on the bed move, and TITO *sits up with an effort, pulling the covers from his face. Groggy and heavily drugged, he looks around, as . . .)*

The curtain falls

ACT TWO

Scene 1

Later that night, about 11 p.m.

There is one striking difference from the last time we saw the suite: the bed is empty and TITO *is gone. In addition, the bathroom and connecting doors are both ajar, and the sitting room/corridor door is in the closed position, but not pulled shut.*

In the darkness, we hear the final, serene moments of the Otello–Desdemona duet, "Gia nella notte densa." As the duet ends, the lights come up, and we hear someone knocking at the sitting room/corridor door.

MAGGIE *(offstage):* It's open.

JULIA *(offstage):* That's odd. (JULIA *and* MAGGIE *enter, cautiously at first. Both are dressed as in the previous scene)* Tito . . . ?

MAGGIE *(calling):* Mr. Merelli . . . ?

JULIA *(into the bedroom):* Tito . . . ?

MAGGIE: I guess he's not back yet.

JULIA *(puzzled):* Apparently not.

(She pulls the connecting door closed)

MAGGIE *(relaxing now; collapsing onto the sofa):* Oh my God. Wasn't he wonderful!

JULIA: Wonderful isn't the word, my dear. He was box office all the way. *(The telephone rings)* I wonder who that could be.

MAGGIE: Maybe it's him.

JULIA *(into the phone):* Hello? . . . No he isn't back yet, I'm

afraid. Who is this, please? *(Startled)* Oh my goodness. Is anything— . . . Julia Leverett. Chairman of the Opera Guild.

MAGGIE: Who is it?

JULIA *(to* MAGGIE): The police.

MAGGIE: Police?!

JULIA *(into the phone):* Is anything wrong, officer? . . . Yes, I was
there.

MAGGIE: What's the matter?

JULIA: Shh! *(into the phone)* Oh dear. I see . . . Well that's good
. . . Oh dear! . . . Oh good . . . Oh dear . . . I certainly will.
Thank you very much. Goodbye.

MAGGIE: Well?

JULIA: It's very sad actually. Apparently some lunatic dressed as
Otello tried to get into the theatre tonight. He said he was Tito
Merelli.

MAGGIE: Oh no.

JULIA: When they wouldn't let him in, he started screaming in
Italian, so the stage manager called the police.

MAGGIE: Did they get him?

JULIA: Well, they arrested him and dragged him off, but he got
away down an alley. Apparently the man's demented. When
they grabbed him he actually hit a policeman.

MAGGIE: Oh my God.

JULIA: They're sending two of their men over to keep an eye out.

MAGGIE: I hope nothing happens.

JULIA: That's all we need at the reception is some lunatic on the rampage. We'll have enough of those already when the Board starts drinking. *(She heads for the door)* I suppose we'd better go. They'll start arriving any minute now.

MAGGIE: Maybe I should wait here. I—I could tell him that you're looking for him. I mean, I just want to be helpful.

JULIA: Of course you do. And I won't tell Max if you don't.

MAGGIE: Max? It's none of his business.

JULIA: Isn't it?

MAGGIE: He didn't even show up tonight.

JULIA *(teasing):* If I see him downstairs, shall I tell him you're looking for him?

MAGGIE: No, thank you.

JULIA: How about Tito?

MAGGIE: Aunt Julia—

JULIA: See you later, my dear.

*(*JULIA *exits, closing the door behind her.* MAGGIE *pauses for a moment, then goes to the telephone and clicks for the operator)*

MAGGIE *(into the phone):* Stage door of the Opera House please . . . Hello, Harry? It's Maggie Saunders . . . Just fine. How are you? . . . Yes it was. It was fabulous. I was just wondering, is . . . is Max around backstage by any chance? . . . *(Disappointed)* Oh . . . Not at all? . . . No, that's all right. It's nothing special. *(The sound of the sitting room/corridor door being unlocked.* MAGGIE *looks up, says quietly)* Thanks, Harry. 'Bye.

(She hangs up. The door opens and MAX *enters. He's still in full costume and make–up. He doesn't see her)*

MAGGIE: Hi.

MAX *(startled)*: *Ciao.*

(MAX *strolls into the room, full of confidence and swagger.* MAG-GIE *is suddenly nervous, being alone with "Tito." She tries to make conversation, but* MAX *isn't helping*)

MAGGIE: I—I hope you don't mind me being here. The door was open—I mean, we knocked first, but you weren't here. Which I guess you know, since you were somewhere else. So then I waited, because I have a message from Aunt Julia. Mrs. Leverett. She's not really my aunt, actually. She's an old friend, but I call her Aunt Julia in case you're wondering. Anyway, she asked me to—to wait here and remind you that she hopes you'll make a speech at the reception. Just a few words, and I'm sure they'd really appreciate it, if you feel like it, which you probably don't, which is understandable, and that's the message.

(Pause)

MAX: Thanks. That's a–very nice of you, eh? To give a–me the massage.

(He realizes his mistake with the word and turns away, rolling his eyes)

MAGGIE: It was nothing really.

MAX: It's a–very sweet.

(Pause. She continues to stare at him)

MAGGIE: So. I—I guess I ought to be going.

MAX: Yeah? That's a–too bad.

MAGGIE: It is?

MAX: Yeah. For me, eh?

MAGGIE *(very pleased)*: Oh. Well. I don't *have* to go. If you don't think so. I mean it's your bedroom. Suite. Rooms. Of course, I'm sure you'd like to just relax a little now and take off my clothes.

World-renowned Italian tenor Tito Merelli (Ron Holgate, at right) consoles
his jealous wife Maria (Tovah Feldshuh) with dramatic visions of a
passionate second honeymoon.

Photo by Martha Swope

Saunders, at right Cleveland's most forceful impresario (Philip Bosco),
envisions the magnitude of the man who would play Otello for his
stagestruck gofer, Max (Victor Garber).

Photo by Martha Swope

Maria (Tovah Feldshuh, at right), Chairman of the Opera Guild Julia
Leverett (Jane Connell) and Saunders (Philip Bosco) try to imagine who
could be behind the bathroom door.

Photo by Martha Swope

The full cast of the original Broadway production (from left to right): Tovah Feldshuh as Maria, J. Smith-Cameron as Maggie, Ron Holgate as Tito, Caroline Lagerfelt as Diana, Victor Garber as Max, Jane Connell as Julia, Philip Bosco as Saunders and Jeff Brooks, kneeling, as the Bellhop.

Photo by Martha Swope

Your clothes! Off. Change your clothes, into something more comfortable. So I probably shouldn't be here for that. If you don't think so.

MAX: Hey. I'm gonna tell you something, it's gonna shock a–you, eh?

MAGGIE: I doubt that.

MAX: It's gonna be a big a–surprise. Okay?

MAGGIE: Okay.

MAX: Tonight, when I'm a–singing my love song to Desdemona . . . I'm a–thinking of you.

MAGGIE: Me?

MAX: *Gia nella notte densa s'estingue ogni clamor. Tuoni la guerra e s'inabissi il mondo se dopo l'ira immensa vien quest'immenso amor.* Now, in the dark a–night, all big sounds, they die away. The guns can a–roar, the whole world can collapse, if, after this immense destruction, there comes this immense a–love.

MAGGIE: Me? *(He kisses her on the lips. She responds. Bells start to ring—all kinds of bells in a long peal of ecstasy.* MAGGIE *breaks and looks up, acknowledging them, then grabs* MAX *in a kiss of passion. They both feel breathless and hot)* I want to bear your children!

MAX: Me too!

(They start kissing again, but MAGGIE *breaks it)*

MAGGIE: But what about your wife?

MAX: My wife? Oh my *wife.* That wife.

MAGGIE: Maria.

MAX: Maria. She . . . she's uh . . . Heh. This is gonna surprise
you, eh? *(Grave)* She's not a–my wife.

MAGGIE: She's not?

MAX: No. She pretends she's a–my wife. She likes to think so, eh?
It's a–very sad.

MAGGIE: Oh, Tito! *(They go at it again, with even more enthusi-
asm, both of them getting hotter by the second. Without warning, there's a knock at the door)* Oh hell!

*(MAGGIE faces front and we see now that her face is smudged all
over with MAX's black make–up)*

MAX: Yeah?!

SAUNDERS *(offstage):* Open up.

MAGGIE: Oh my God! It's my father!

*(She runs to the mirror to compose herself—and sees her face and
screams. Then she pulls a hankie from her purse and tries to get
the make–up off)*

MAX *(buying time):* Who's the–ere?

SAUNDERS *(offstage):* It's me.

MAX: Who is "me," please?

SAUNDERS *(offstage):* Who do you think it is, you jackass! Now
open the door!

*(MAGGIE has finished now as best she can. MAX looks at her and
she nods "Okay")*

MAX *(opening the door):* Ciao.

*(SAUNDERS enters carrying white tie and tails for MAX on a
hanger)*

SAUNDERS: Where have you been?! I've been looking all over— Maggie!

MAGGIE *(shielding her face):* Hi, Daddy.

SAUNDERS: What are you doing here?

MAGGIE: I—I just came up to deliver a message to Mr. Merelli.

SAUNDERS: Oh. Oh I see. To Mr. Merelli.

MAGGIE: Aunt Julia wants him to speak at the reception.

SAUNDERS: Well, we'll have to see about that now, won't we? I'm sure that Mr. Merelli is awfully tired. Aren't you?

MAX: Hm? Yeah. Sure. *(He yawns)*

MAGGIE: Well . . . I guess I ought to be going then.

SAUNDERS: What a good idea.

MAGGIE: It was nice meeting you, Mr. Merelli. I hope to see you again some time.

MAX: Me too, eh?

MAGGIE: *Soon.*

MAX: Soon?

MAGGIE *(nodding hard at the door):* You certainly *unlocked* the *door* to our hearts this evening.

MAX: Thanks.

MAGGIE: And will again, I'm sure.

MAX *(not getting it):* I hope a–so, eh?

MAGGIE: So I won't even say goodbye. Just au revoir.

MAX: *Ciao.* (MAGGIE *exits.* MAX *closes the door; in his own voice)* Well?

SAUNDERS: Max, Max, Max. We did it, you crazy bastard!

MAX: We?

SAUNDERS *(exploding):* A complete triumph! They floated, they suffered, they cried their eyes out.

MAX: I guess I was okay then.

SAUNDERS: Max. Let me put it this way. I owe you one.

MAX: No you don't. You owe me several.

SAUNDERS: You're right. I do. And if there's any little favor you can think of, Max, any trifling thing—

MAX: Next season.

SAUNDERS: Hm?

MAX: I thought I'd start out next season with Don Jose in *Carmen.*

SAUNDERS: Oh.

MAX: Then Rodolfo in *La Bohème,* then finish off with something lighter, like *Die Fledermaus.*

SAUNDERS: Max—

MAX: Sir?

SAUNDERS: It just so happens, I have another idea. An inspiration. A flash of genius. You're going to love it.

MAX: Yeah?

SAUNDERS *(smiling cunningly):* Verdi's *Requiem.*

MAX: I don't get it.

SAUNDERS: Requiem! Mass for the dead. Who is dead, Max?

MAX: Tito! I almost forgot.

SAUNDERS: Well I didn't, and I have it all figured out. Tomorrow morning we arrive together. We knock at the door, no answer, so we get the manager. He lets us in and "Oh–my–God, the man is dead! Tito! Tito! What have you done?" Too late. He's gone. Within the hour, it hits the wire service and by Monday we've got every newspaper and magazine in the country here. So—I call a press conference. I make a short and touching statement: "We, of the Cleveland Grand Opera Company, we who were graced by the final warblings of that immortal voice which is no more, we will honour the memory of Il Stupendo a week from today at eight o'clock with a single performance of Mr. Merelli's favorite and sadly appropriate work of music—Verdi's *Requiem.*"

MAX: Was that his favorite?

SAUNDERS: How the hell should I know?!

MAX: Sorry.

SAUNDERS: The point is, you idiot, it'll put us on the map! The publicity will be incredible. I couldn't have planned the whole thing better if I'd strangled him myself. Now guess, Max, guess who will sing the tenor solos in the *Requiem.* Hm?

MAX: Me?

SAUNDERS: You.

MAX: Thanks.

SAUNDERS: Now look, I've got to get downstairs to that stupid reception, so here's the drill. Put this on, *(handing him the white tie and tails)* turn back into Max. Then wait in here, with the door locked, and do not, under any circumstances, let anyone in. I'll make Tito's excuses downstairs, and then, when the reception's over, I'll come back up and we'll both leave. All right? Good. Now go change.

(He heads for the door)

MAX: Uh . . . sir?

SAUNDERS: Max?!

MAX: I, uh . . . I just want to say that I—I really liked him, and I don't think you ever quite realized what a . . . a really nice man he was. I mean, before he died.

SAUNDERS: Max. Believe me—I loved him like a brother. But there's nothing we can do for him now. It's just too late.

MAX: I guess so.

SAUNDERS: If it's any comfort to you, Max, just remember—from here on out, it's clear sailing. Absolutely nothing can go wrong.

(SAUNDERS *exits, closing the door behind him.*

Simultaneously, the bedroom/corridor door bursts open and TITO *enters. He, too, is dressed as Otello, in exactly the same costume and make-up that* MAX *is wearing.* TITO *is in a state of panic. Exhausted and bedraggled, he pants heavily from running. His eyes dart madly in every direction as he leans against the door, gasping for air.*

Also simultaneously, a siren wails from the street below as though a police car is pulling up at the hotel. MAX *walks to the window and looks down.* TITO *hears the siren and dives into the closet, closing the door behind him.* MAX *shrugs and heads for the bedroom. As he reaches the connecting door, he hesitates and braces himself)*

MAX: Poor Tito. *(He sighs, covers his eyes and enters the room, heading for the bathroom.* MAX *doesn't want to see* TITO's *body. He couldn't bear it. And yet, he can't help himself. He separates his fingers and glances at the bed; then covers his eyes again and turns away. Poor Tito! He continues into the bathroom and closes the door. Offstage)* Oh my God! (MAX *runs out of the bathroom without the white tie and tails and closing the door behind him and stares at the bed, dumbfounded. He tears away*

the covers, looks under the bed and around the room. No Tito!)
Oh my God!! *(He hesitates for a split second, then runs out of the bedroom into the corridor, closing the door behind him)* MIS-TER SAUNDERS!!

(Pause. Slowly the closet door opens and TITO *emerges. He looks around and listens. Not a sound. He sighs heavily, then totters cautiously through the bedroom and into the sitting room. He looks around the room. He feels certain now that he's safe at last and sinks onto the sofa and closes his eyes. At which point,* JULIA *enters through the sitting room/corridor door and sees* TITO *from the back, sitting quietly on the sofa. She smiles; then walks silently into the room and covers his eyes with her hands)*

JULIA: Guess who?

TITO: YIY!!

(He bounds to his feet and stares at her)

JULIA: Now, aren't you ashamed of yourself. Sitting here quietly enjoying yourself, while everyone downstairs is simply dying to meet you.

TITO: Excuse me please, but who are you?

JULIA: You're angry with me, aren't you?

TITO: Angry?

JULIA: Here I am, haranguing you about the reception when I haven't even told you how magnificent you were tonight. Tito. My dear man. *(Sitting and leaning back seductively, lowering her voice to the bass range)* How can I ever thank you?

TITO: For what?

JULIA: For what? For what you did this evening!

TITO: I didn't do nothing! It wasn't me!

JULIA: No it wasn't you. You're right. It was Otello. There, onstage, in flesh and blood. It was beauty and it was life. It was love and it was pain. And as I sat there in the theatre, watching you tonight, hanging on your every note, I thought to myself: Now, at this moment, I am hearing the greatest performance of any opera star that has ever lived!

TITO: I was good, eh?

JULIA: Words cannot express it.

TITO: I think I'm a–gonna siddown, okay? *(He does)*

JULIA: You poor thing. You've had a bad day, haven't you?

TITO: Yeah.

JULIA: Of course you have, and you've been very brave. But, Tito, dear Tito. You will come down to the reception, won't you? For just a few minutes?

TITO: No. I done think so.

JULIA: But, Tito, you promised me!

TITO: I did?

JULIA: Tito Merelli. I'm surprised at you. How could you possibly disappoint me like this? Me. Julia.

TITO: I'm sorry, eh?

JULIA: And I'm sorry, too. For I simply will not take no for an answer. Do you understand? I will not budge from this spot until you agree. Not one inch. *(She folds her arms and stands firm)* There are times, I'm afraid, when one simply has to apply the iron glove in the velvet hand. Especially if one hopes to get the bird.

TITO *(thinking):* Okay. I give up.

JULIA: You do?

TITO: Yeah.

JULIA: Oh, Tito, you're wonderful! I knew you wouldn't let us down. Let's go!

TITO: No. Hey. *(He turns on the charm and takes her hand)* Julia. I'm a–tired, eh? I need a few minutes to, uh, get off a–my feet, wash a–my face. Okay, Julia?

JULIA *(aroused):* Oh, my dearest, dearest Tito. You've made me so very happy. I only wish there was something I could do for you. *(Lowering her voice and trying again)* Can you think of anything?

TITO: Yeah. Go.

JULIA: I understand. Poor baby. You need some time alone. *(He ushers her to the door)* Every minute shall seem an hour, and every hour a second. And so I fly.

(She exits, closing the door)

TITO: Jesus Christ! *(He thinks for a moment about what to do— then springs into action. He rushes into the bedroom, grabs his suitcase and puts it on the bed to pack. Then a thought strikes him)* Train station. *(He hurries into the sitting room toward the phone book. He finds it and rifles through it searching for "train station")* Train, train, train. (At this moment, the sitting room/ corridor door opens and* DIANA *enters, wearing the slinkiest, most inviting dress imaginable. She closes the door quietly. By this time,* TITO *has found the appropriate page and heads back towards the bedroom, scanning the column)* Tractors. Trailers. Trophies.

DIANA: Hi there. (TITO *stops dead. He looks at* DIANA—*and drops the phone book to the floor)* Surprised to see me? *(He shakes his head "yes" and wheezes)* I told you I might drop in. Didn't you believe me? *(He shakes his head "no" and wheezes)* Are you all right?

TITO: Dry . . . dry throat.

DIANA: Then perhaps I should order some champagne. What do you think?

TITO: Sure. Great.

DIANA: May I use the phone? (DIANA *walks to the telephone.* TITO *watches her, fascinated. She picks up the phone and clicks for the operator. Into the phone)* Room service, please. *(As she waits, she smiles at* TITO. *He smiles back. Into the phone)* Yes, I'd like to order a bottle of champagne. *(To* TITO) Is Mumm all right?

TITO: She's fine, thank you.

DIANA *(into the phone):* Yes. That'll be fine. *(She hangs up)* Well. You certainly are a fast operator, I must say. I barely know you, and here we are, alone in your hotel room with a bottle of champagne on the way up.

TITO: I'm just a tricky guy, eh?

DIANA: Come here.

TITO: Huh?

DIANA: Come here. *(She sits on the sofa and motions him to sit beside her. He does, cautiously. She faces him directly)* Tito. Can I ask you a question?

TITO: Sure. Hey.

DIANA: I want you to be totally honest with me. All right? Do you promise?

TITO: Cross a–my heart.

DIANA: Brutal, if necessary.

TITO: Nooo . . .

DIANA: Yes. Please.

TITO: Okay.

(Pause)

DIANA: Was I good tonight?

TITO: Good?

DIANA: I'm sure it's difficult to make any lasting judgments, after having done it with me only once. But would you say I was . . . exciting tonight?

TITO *(trying to work it out):* We spent a–some time together, eh?

DIANA: We certainly did.

TITO: Yeah . . .

DIANA: Now I want the truth. Just take the big moment at the end. Would you say it was something special? *(No answer)* I can take it, believe me, Tito. I'm a professional.

TITO: A pro—? Oh my God. A *professional!*

DIANA *(hurt):* You don't think so?

TITO: No I do! I promise!

DIANA: Well then? How was I? *(Pause)* Tito?

TITO: I'm trying to remember!

DIANA *(bitterly):* I suppose you're telling me I was no good.

TITO: No! Hey! You—you were great! You were fantastic!

DIANA: You're only saying that—

TITO: No I swear! You—you were unbelievable! It went a–by so fast, I can hardly remember.

DIANA: Oh, Tito. Do you mean it?

TITO: Yeah. Sure.

DIANA: Thank God. I'm so relieved.

TITO: Heh. This, uh, profession. You take it a–pretty serious, eh?

DIANA: It's all I've ever wanted to be since I was a little girl. Isn't that awful?

TITO: It's terrible.

DIANA: Of course my mother was in the business.

TITO: Ah.

DIANA: And my father was too.

TITO: You father?

DIANA: I guess you could say it's in my blood.

TITO: You got something in you blood?!

DIANA: Does it show?

TITO: No! No! You look–a fine.

DIANA: And you thought I was good tonight. I mean really, really good?

TITO: Oh yeah. Great.

DIANA: You have no idea what this means to me, Tito. Coming from you.

TITO: Heh, thanks.

DIANA: I was so afraid you were disappointed. I mean, it's just so hard to tell with all those people there.

TITO *(after a slight pause):* People?

DIANA: You really are incredible, aren't you. You've had so much experience, you don't even notice them. I think that's wonderful.

TITO: People?!

DIANA: Tito.

TITO: Eh?

DIANA: Now, Tito, just supposing that I really am as good as you think. And supposing that I have the confidence and the stamina to make it in the big time, in New York . . .

TITO: Yeah?

DIANA: I was wondering if, perhaps, you'd like to introduce me to some of your friends. Is that possible, Tito?

TITO: Hey. I'm not so sure, eh?

DIANA: Producers. Directors. The ones that matter. What about your agent?

TITO: My agent, she's a woman.

DIANA: So? That's all right with me.

TITO: It is?

DIANA: Of course! I wouldn't care if she was a kangaroo! The important thing is whether she's good or not. Right?!

TITO: I guess.

DIANA: All I'd need with her is five minutes. And if she doesn't think I'm special, at least I tried. I had a chance! Tito?

TITO: Hey. I do my best, okay?

DIANA: You will?

TITO: If that's a–what you want.

DIANA: Tito. How can I ever thank you?

TITO: My pleasure, eh?

DIANA: It will be. I promise. *(She kisses him, passionately. Almost at once we hear a knock at the sitting room/corridor door)* Oh see who it is!

(TITO *gets up, reluctantly, and goes to the door*)

TITO: Who is, please?

MAGGIE *(offstage):* It's me. Maggie.

TITO *(to DIANA, whispering):* Who's Moggie?

DIANA: She's Henry's daughter. I suppose she wants your autograph or something.

MAGGIE *(offstage):* Open up!

TITO: *Minuto!*

DIANA *(taking her purse):* Go ahead, but just get rid of her as soon as you can. I'll slip into something more comfortable. How does that sound?

TITO: I like it.

DIANA: Keep warm.

(She throws him a kiss and exits into the bathroom, closing the door. TITO watches her go, then closes the connecting door)

MAGGIE *(offstage):* Tito! (TITO *opens the door to the corridor.* MAGGIE *hurries in and quickly closes the door. Breathless)* I slipped out during one of the speeches, so I don't think anybody noticed. Of course I might have been going to the ladies' room or out for a walk, I mean there's nothing wrong with that, except I think I looked suspicious.

TITO: How do you do.

MAGGIE: A lot better, now that I'm here. Are you all right?

TITO: I'm a–fine, thank you.

MAGGIE: Good.

(She advances into the room and takes a breath)

TITO: So.

MAGGIE: So.

TITO: I think I know why you come, eh?

MAGGIE: I guess you do.

TITO: You want a–my autograph.

MAGGIE: Is that what you call it in Italian?

TITO: In Italian is *autografo.*

(MAGGIE turns her back on TITO, afraid to look at him. During the following, she doesn't see what TITO's doing—which is looking around on the tables for a pen and a piece of paper)

MAGGIE: And what's the word for "love" in Italian? *Amore?*

TITO *(searching):* Hey, that's good. You speak a–the language, eh?

MAGGIE: I never would have believed that anything like this could have ever happened.

TITO: Life is funny, eh?

MAGGIE: It certainly is.

(By now, TITO has found the pen and paper and sits on the sofa, facing away from MAGGIE, to use the coffee table to write on)

TITO: So, what would you like me to say, eh? *(Writing)* "Moggie . . ."

MAGGIE: Tito . . .

TITO: I get to that.

MAGGIE *(still facing away from him):* Tito . . . Before we go any
further, I want you to know that I've never done anything like
this before.

TITO: No?

MAGGIE: No. Which doesn't mean that I regret it. Not for a second.

TITO: Hey. I done mind. Honest.

MAGGIE *(pale):* You "don't mind?"

(They face each other)

TITO: Is no big deal, eh? I do it all the time.

MAGGIE: Well. Then maybe we should just forget all about it.

TITO: No! Hey. For me is a pleasure. A privilege. It makes me feel
proud, eh?

MAGGIE: Do you mean that?

(They turn away from each other again)

TITO: Sure. And I'm gonna make it a–very special. Just a–for you.
(He reads) "Moggie."

MAGGIE: I *want* it to be special, Tito! I want it to be everything
I've ever dreamed of!

TITO: Hey. I do my best, okay? (MAGGIE *unzips her dress and pulls
it down around her. Reading)* "Moggie." *(Writing)* "A very

special a–person . . ." (MAGGIE's *dress drops to the floor, and she steps out of it. Writing)* "And beautiful to look at."

MAGGIE: Thank you.

TITO *(signing with a flourish):* "Merelli." So. Now you gonna have a–my name forever.

MAGGIE *(hushed; thrilled):* Your name? Forever?

TITO *(feeling the paper):* Should last pretty good.

(MAGGIE *turns and looks at him. It's a dream come true)*

MAGGIE: Oh, Tito!

(He turns in surprise at the tone of her voice and sees her in her underwear)

TITO: YIY! *(He drops the pen and paper)*

MAGGIE: I'm yours. All yours.

(She goes straight for him and pushes him backwards onto the sofa, kissing his face and neck)

TITO: Moggie!

MAGGIE: Tito! *(If he could have stopped her, it's too late now. She's all over him. He's struggling for air—when without warning, there's a knock at the door. Very insistent. They both freeze)* Holy cow! Are you expecting anybody?

TITO: No.

SAUNDERS *(offstage):* Max?!

TITO: Max?

MAGGIE *(horrified):* Oh my God! It's Daddy!

TITO: Daddy?

MAGGIE *(jumping up):* If he finds me here like this, he'll kill you!

TITO: Keel?

MAGGIE: He'll go crazy! I've got to hide!

SAUNDERS *(offstage, knocking):* Max?!

(MAGGIE heads towards the bedroom)

TITO: No!

(Too late. MAGGIE opens the door and enters the bedroom. TITO runs in after her)

MAGGIE: Closet or bathroom?!

TITO: Closet!

MAGGIE: You're right! *(She runs to the closet and opens the door)* Just tell him you haven't seen me!

TITO: I haven't seen you.

(She kisses him quickly, then disappears into the closet, closing the door. At which point, the bathroom door opens and DIANA enters. She wears a towel)

DIANA: Is she gone yet?

TITO: Not yet.

DIANA: Well, get rid of her!

TITO: I do my best.

DIANA: Perhaps I'll take a bubble bath. Then you can join me.

TITO: Bubble? I wone be long.

(She exits back into the bathroom, closing the door. TITO sighs, then runs into the sitting room, closing the connecting door as he goes; then runs to the corridor door and opens it)

SAUNDERS *(offstage):* MAX!

TITO: *Ciao.*

(SAUNDERS *glares at him and enters*)

SAUNDERS: What are you *doing* in here?!

TITO *(shrugging innocently):* Nothing.

SAUNDERS: You haven't even changed yet.

TITO: Change?

SAUNDERS: I told you to change! For God's sake, you'll ruin everything!

TITO: I'm a–sorry, eh? *(Trying to get him out)* Thanks a–for coming.

SAUNDERS: Will you cut the phony accent! I'm not amused.

TITO: You done like it?

SAUNDERS: Look. I know you think this is great fun. You're Il Stupendo. Big star. Hot stuff—

TITO: Yeah.

SAUNDERS: But it's not the time to fool around! Just imagine what would happen if anybody found out. My blood runs cold when I even—*(He stops in his tracks. He's staring at the floor—at* MAGGIE's *dress. He picks it up and holds it out, confirming that it is, indeed, a woman's dress. He looks at* TITO) Is there a woman in here?

TITO: Yeah.

SAUNDERS: Are you out of your mind?!!

TITO: I'm not so sure.

SAUNDERS: You're really having a field day, aren't you?

TITO *(shrugging):* Heh . . .

SAUNDERS *(lowering his voice):* Can she hear us?

TITO: I dunno.

SAUNDERS: That explains the accent.

TITO: It does?

(SAUNDERS *sidles over to the kitchenette)*

SAUNDERS *(whispering):* Is she in there?

TITO: No.

SAUNDERS *(looking around the room):* Well, where is she?

TITO: The bathroom.

SAUNDERS: The bathroom?! Are you crazy?! What about the body?!

TITO: The body?

SAUNDERS: The body!

TITO: Like I said, she's in the bathroom.

SAUNDERS: Not that body. The other body.

TITO: Oh. *(Resigned)* The closet.

SAUNDERS: The closet? You stuffed the body in the closet?

TITO: Is a big closet.

SAUNDERS: Look. I would be the first to admit that you deserve a little reward for all you've been through.

TITO: Thanks.

SAUNDERS: But it's not the time!

TITO: Okay.

SAUNDERS: Now first of all, I want you to get rid of the girl—

TITO: Which one?

SAUNDERS: There's more than one?

TITO *(sheepishly):* Two.

SAUNDERS: You've got two girls in there?

TITO: Yeah.

SAUNDERS: I knew you had potential, but this is incredible.

TITO: Thanks.

SAUNDERS: Look. I'm impressed. All right? I'm very impressed. But get them the hell out of here!! Do you have any idea who's downstairs right now?

TITO: No.

SAUNDERS: The police! And they're asking questions!

TITO *(croaking):* Police?

SAUNDERS: That's what I came up to tell you. They're looking for some madman who tried to break into the theatre tonight. In costume!

TITO: Police?

(A knock at the sitting room/corridor door)

SAUNDERS: Oh hell. That could be them. *(Lowering his voice)* All right. Here's the story. You're still Tito. You came back from the

theatre and went straight to your room. *(During the following,*
SAUNDERS *leads* TITO *to the connecting door, to hide him in the*
bedroom) You haven't seen anything unusual, whatsoever. And
whatever we do, we keep them away from the closet! *(He closes*
the connecting door, leaving TITO *in the bedroom. Another*
knock at the door) Coming!

(He opens the door. MAX, *still dressed as Otello, rushes in)*

MAX: I've got to talk to you! *(He closes the door)*

*(*SAUNDERS *is speechless and reels backwards. Meanwhile,* TITO,
still in the bedroom, leans against the connecting wall, arm out-
stretched; MAX *does the same in the sitting room. They unknow-*
ingly create a mirror image)

SAUNDERS: This is no time for jokes, you idiot!!!

MAX: Jokes?

SAUNDERS: Are you out of your mind?! What's the matter with
you?!

MAX: What did *I* do?!

SAUNDERS: This whole thing could blow up any second!!

MAX: I know!

SAUNDERS: Well, who was at the door?!

MAX: What door?

SAUNDERS: That door! Who was knocking?!

MAX: Me.

SAUNDERS: Before that!

MAX: How should I know?

SAUNDERS: You were there!

MAX: Where?!

SAUNDERS: At the door!

MAX: What door?!

SAUNDERS: *That door!!! (Pause. They're at an impasse. At this point,* TITO *opens the bedroom/corridor door and exits, pulling the door closed quietly behind him.* SAUNDERS *goes on reasonably; restraining himself)* Max. A minute ago, you were standing here and I was talking to you. There was a knock at the door, and I said, "That may be the police—"

MAX: It wasn't me.

SAUNDERS: I know that!

MAX: I mean, in here!

SAUNDERS: Max—

MAX: I was downstairs, looking for you! When I couldn't find you, I came back up!

SAUNDERS: You were looking for me?

MAX: Yes!

SAUNDERS: Why were you looking for me?

MAX: That's what I want to tell you! He's gone.

SAUNDERS: Who?

MAX: Tito! He's gone!

SAUNDERS: Max! We all have to go sometime!

MAX: I mean he's not on the bed!! He disappeared!! Look. You told me to go change and you went downstairs. I walked in there and I tried not to look, but I couldn't help it, so I looked at the bed and he wasn't there.

SAUNDERS: He's in the closet.

MAX: Who told you that?

SAUNDERS: You—*(He freezes. He figures it out)* Oh my God. He's alive.

MAX: Do you really think so?

SAUNDERS: I was standing here talking to him!!! *(He bolts to the connecting door and throws it open. He looks around the bedroom and sees that it's empty)* He's gone.

MAX: But he's alive. That's terrific!

SAUNDERS: You moron! He could ruin everything! *(A knock at the sitting room/corridor door.* SAUNDERS *and* MAX *freeze.* SAUNDERS *goes on, lowering his voice)* It's either him or the police.

MAX: Oh great.

SAUNDERS: Whatever I say, just play along.

(MAX *sits on the sofa as* SAUNDERS *walks to the corridor door and opens it. The* BELLHOP *enters, carrying an ice bucket, a bottle of champagne and two glasses)*

BELLHOP: Nightcap, anyone?

SAUNDERS: Oh no!!

BELLHOP: Mr. Merelli! Oh, sir, I know how tired you must be and I won't take up much of your time, but I simply must tell you how magnificent you were tonight. You were wonderful!

MAX: Thanks.

BELLHOP: I'll never forget it as long as I live.

MAX: You liked it, eh?

BELLHOP: I adored every note.

MAX: What exactly did you like a–best?

SAUNDERS *(to* MAX): Not now!!

BELLHOP *(dramatically):* When you realized that she was inno-
cent, but it was too late. *Oh, Desdemona. Morta. Morta. Morta.* It
was so beautiful!

SAUNDERS: Who the hell ordered champagne?!

BELLHOP: He did.

MAX: I did?

SAUNDERS: You did?

BELLHOP: That's what they told me downstairs.

SAUNDERS: Oh yes of course. I remember now. *(To* MAX) The
champagne.

MAX: Oh yeah. I forget, eh?

BELLHOP: And guess what? It's on the house, and *I* arranged it.

SAUNDERS: Well, that's very nice of you.

BELLHOP: I did it for *him.*

SAUNDERS: Well, now you've done it, so get out.

BELLHOP *(ignoring* SAUNDERS): Is there anything else I can do for
you, Mr. Merelli?

MAX: I done think so. Thanks.

SAUNDERS: Out.

BELLHOP: Well, if you want anything, just pick up the phone. I'm
on all night.

SAUNDERS: Out!!

BELLHOP *(unruffled, to* MAX): I'll see you later. *(He frowns)* Goodbye, Henry. *(He exits, closing the door)*

SAUNDERS: All right, now listen. Here's the plan. Number one, you change. And do it this time!

MAX: Yes, sir.

SAUNDERS: I'll go find Tito and explain everything. And then, if I have to, I'll pay him off.

(He goes to the corridor door)

MAX: Sir? Since we're not doing the *Requiem,* can I do the *Carmen?*

SAUNDERS: Change!

MAX: Yes, sir.

(SAUNDERS *exits.* MAX *walks into the bedroom, leaving the connecting door open and heads straight for the bathroom. He walks into the bathroom and closes the door. Pause. A cry from* MAX, *as the door swings open,* MAX *holding the handle for dear life.* DIANA, *still in her towel, yanks him back in and the door slams. Repeat. Bubbles each time. Silence for a moment; then the closet door opens and* MAGGIE *cautiously emerges. She wears* TITO'S *trench coat over her underwear)*

MAGGIE *(in a whisper):* Tito? *(There's a yelp from the bathroom and* MAGGIE *is startled by it. Then she realizes that he must be using the bathroom)* Oh. *(She calls quietly)* Sorry! *(She sighs with relief and goes into the sitting room, smiling happily. Then she notices the champagne)* Oh, Tito! Champagne! *(She picks up one of the glasses admiringly. She notices a speck of dirt on it. She picks up the other glass, decides that both glasses need washing, and walks into the kitchenette, happily humming a popular tune. As* MAGGIE *exits, the bathroom door crashes open and* MAX *reels out, breathing heavily.* DIANA *follows him out still wearing her towel)*

DIANA: Now, don't go 'way, I have a little surprise for you. I'll be right back.

(She exits into the bathroom and closes the door. MAX *catches his breath, then staggers into the sitting room, closing the connecting door behind him.* MAGGIE, *who's heard the door, enters from the kitchenette without the glasses)*

MAGGIE: Darling. *(She shrugs the trench coat off her shoulders and it falls to the floor)* Alone at last. (MAX *falls to his knees, speechless and exhausted)* You poor thing, you look tired. You've had a rough day, haven't you? (MAX *shakes his head "yes."* MAGGIE *goes to him)* Now, don't you worry. I'm going to make it all better. *(She leads him to the sofa and pushes him on to it)* You'll see.

(MAX *is flat on his back.* MAGGIE'*s on top of him, kissing him passionately, which is when the bedroom/corridor door opens and* TITO *rushes in, closing the door quickly, but quietly. He's on the lam and breathing heavily. He runs to his suitcase, grabs it and turns to go when* DIANA *enters from the bathroom. She wears a nightie which is extremely sexy.* TITO *sees her, freezes, and drops the suitcase)*

DIANA: Well? Do you like it? (TITO *shakes his head "yes")* I thought you might.

TITO: Heh . . .

DIANA: You poor thing, you look tired. You've had a rough day, haven't you? (TITO *shakes his head "yes."* DIANA *goes to him)* Now don't you worry. I'm going to make it all better. You'll see.

(She pushes him onto the bed and climbs on top of him, kissing him passionately)

MAX *(in the sitting room):* Shall we turn off a–the lights?

DIANA *(in the bedroom):* I like it with the lights on.

MAGGIE *(in the sitting room):* If that's all right with you.

TITO *(in the bedroom):* It's a–fine with me.

(Both couples go at it again, with increasing passion. And as they continue, the lights fade to black.

As the lights fade, music comes up: the final moments of the tenor–soprano duet "Da quel di che t'incontrai" from Donizetti's Linda di Chamounix. *It's a love song that begins with a lilt, then breaks into a gallop, building to a final cry of joy from the soprano)*

Scene 2

Fifteen minutes later.

When the duet is over, the lights come up. Both couples have just finished making love. DIANA *is propped up in bed;* MAGGIE *is sitting on the sofa.* TITO *and* MAX *are both pulling their boots back on. Obviously, each couple is unaware of the other couple in the adjoining room.*

MAGGIE: It was even better than I thought it would be. I guess that's because you're Italian.

MAX: I guess so, eh?

DIANA: I bet you don't feel tired anymore, do you?

*(*TITO *sways from exhaustion. He's about to collapse)*

TITO: No . . . no . . .

DIANA: I must look awful. I think I'd better do some reconstruction. *(She leaves the bed and heads for the bathroom)* I won't be long.

TITO: Take a–you time, eh?

*(*DIANA *exits into the bathroom and closes the door.* TITO *falls backwards onto the bed in utter exhaustion)*

MAGGIE: I think I'd like some champagne now. Want some?

MAX: Why not, eh?

MAGGIE: It was so sweet of you to think of it. But then you think of everything, don't you?

MAX: It's the way I am, eh?

MAGGIE: You pop the cork, I'll dry the glasses. *(Sexy)* Maybe it'll put us in the mood again.

MAX: Could be.

(She exits into the kitchenette. The moment she's gone, MAX *breaks into song—the "Toreador Song" from* Carmen. *He dances to the sofa and begins opening the champagne.*

After a moment, TITO *sits up in bed and listens. He hears the singing and it sounds close by. He cocks his head, to listen better, then looks towards the sitting room. As* MAX *continues opening the bottle,* TITO *gets up from the bed and goes to the connecting door. He listens; then opens the door, cautiously and silently, to find out who's in there.* MAX *is facing towards the opposite wall and doesn't see—or hear—the door open.*

TITO *takes a step into the sitting room and sees* MAX—*or rather, he sees himself opening a bottle of champagne and singing. He freezes, speechless. He looks down at himself, then back at* MAX. *He now realizes there's a fair possibility that he's lost his mind. And if he hasn't lost his mind, he doesn't want an explanation; he just wants out.*

TITO *steps back into the bedroom, leaving the connecting door open. Then he runs to his suitcase, grabs it, and runs from the room, out the corridor door, closing it behind him.*

As that door closes, the bathroom door opens and DIANA *enters the bedroom, still in her nightie. She sees that the bedroom is empty but notices that the connecting door is open. She walks to the door and sees* MAX—*who is still opening the champagne.*

As DIANA *enters the sitting room from the bedroom,* MAGGIE *enters from the kitchenette, holding the glasses)*

DIANA: The champagne!

MAGGIE *(simultaneously):* All set! (MAX *is speechless.* MAGGIE *turns to* DIANA) What are you doing here?!

DIANA: I was about to ask you the same thing.

MAGGIE: This happens to be a private party.

DIANA: It certainly is, so scram.

MAGGIE: Tito, tell her to leave!

MAX *(to* DIANA): A–leave!

DIANA: Tell *her* that, you idiot!

MAGGIE: Tito, what is she doing here?!

MAX: I—I—I—I—I—I—

MAGGIE *(to* DIANA): How long have you been here?

DIANA: About a half hour.

MAGGIE: That's impossible. *I've* been here a half hour.

DIANA: Yes, I know. I was here when you arrived. He said he'd get rid of you as soon as possible.

MAGGIE: Tito. Did you know she was in there?

MAX: I—I—I—I—I—

MAGGIE *(pale):* You did.

MAX: It's not a–what you think, eh?

MAGGIE: How could you do this?! After what you said to me?!

DIANA: Never trust a man in tights.

MAGGIE: You louse. *(Approaching him)* You . . . you crumb.

DIANA: Just what I was thinking.

MAX: Hey! I gotta go now.

(He pushes them back onto the sofa and bolts away)

MAGGIE: Stop him! Don't let him out!

(DIANA *runs to the corridor door to block it)*

MAX: Hey!

(He throws the champagne in the air and MAGGIE *catches it; then he hands the vase of flowers to* DIANA *and darts towards the bedroom)*

DIANA: Get him! (MAX *runs into the bedroom, pursued by both women)* Block the door!

MAGGIE: Grab him!

DIANA: I'm trying!

MAGGIE: Stop him!

(MAX *rushes into the bathroom and closes the door. The women rush to the door and try to open it. Too late)*

DIANA: It's locked!

(MAGGIE *grabs the doorknob and rattles it violently)*

MAGGIE: Come out of there, you—you—rat!

DIANA: It's no use.

MAGGIE: Coward!!

DIANA: Save your breath. I know his type.

(Pause. MAGGIE *sighs in frustration)*

MAGGIE: Now what do we do?

DIANA: I don't know about you, but I'm getting dressed.

MAGGIE: Good idea.

(MAGGIE *glares at the bathroom door, then walks into the sitting room to retrieve her dress. Meanwhile,* DIANA *looks around the room for her dress, then remembers she left it in the bathroom. She walks to the bathroom door)*

DIANA: Tito. My dress is in there. *(No response.* DIANA *knocks on the door)* Tito. I need my dress. I promise I won't hurt you. *(No response)* GIVE ME THE GODDAMN DRESS OR I'LL KILL YOU!!! *(In a single action, the bathroom door opens, the dress flies out, the door slams shut and is locked again from the inside)* Thank you, Tito.

(The women get dressed in silence; both in the bedroom)

MAGGIE: I wouldn't have believed it was possible. He seemed so nice.

DIANA: He is nice. He's just a little tricky, that's all.

MAGGIE: Does this sort of thing happen very often?

DIANA: Yes and no. I've been two–timed before, but never with quite so much flair. I mean, you've got to hand it to him.

MAGGIE: I did. That's the problem.

DIANA: Hook? (DIANA *turns and* MAGGIE *hooks up the back)* Thank you.

MAGGIE: My pleasure.

(At this moment, the sitting room/corridor door opens and MARIA *enters, carrying her vanity case. She leaves the door ajar)*

MARIA: One a–more chance, eh? One a–more chance and that's it!

*(*MAGGIE *and* DIANA *both hear* MARIA *and look at each other, puzzled.* DIANA *enters the sitting room)*

DIANA: Oh my God, he's got another one!

*(*MARIA *is startled; then glares suspiciously at* DIANA*)*

MARIA: Who are you?!

DIANA: A friend of the family. Who are you?

MARIA: The family.

DIANA: Tito's wife?

MARIA: That's a–right.

DIANA *(calling):* Maggie, dear. Guess who's here.

MARIA: I'm gonna keel 'im.

DIANA: We know just how you feel.

MAGGIE *(as she enters the sitting room):* Hi.

MARIA: You again.

DIANA: You've met before?

MAGGIE: Just once. In the closet.

DIANA: You realize of course that she's Tito's wife.

MAGGIE: Yeah. Only she isn't really his wife. Tito told me. She likes to pretend she is, and he plays along because he doesn't want to hurt her feelings.

MARIA: Tito tell you this?

MAGGIE: Of course.

MARIA: I'm gonna keel 'im. I swear before God, on everything that's a–holy, I'm gonna strangle him!

DIANA: She sounds like his wife.

MARIA: With my bare hands!!

DIANA: She's his wife.

MAGGIE: But he *said* . . . *(She realizes)* Oh my God.

MARIA: Where is he? (MAGGIE *and* DIANA *look at each other)* Where is he?!!

MAGGIE & DIANA *(together):* The bathroom.

(MARIA *stalks into the bedroom, towards the bathroom door.* DIANA *and* MAGGIE *follow her)*

DIANA: He locked himself in.

MAGGIE: He won't come out.

DIANA: We tried!

MAGGIE: You're sure you're his wife?!

(MARIA *growls in response. Then she tries the door, without success)*

MARIA: Tito. It's Maria.

MAX *(offstage):* Oh no!

MARIA *(banging on the door with her fist):* Open the door right now cause I'm gonna keel you!! You hear me, you big–a pig! Open the door!!

(As MARIA *bangs and hollers, there's an eruption of overlapping voices as* TITO *runs in through the sitting room/corridor door pursued by* SAUNDERS, JULIA *and the* BELLHOP*)*

TITO: Help!

SAUNDERS: Stop!

JULIA: Tito! Please!

TITO: Help!

BELLHOP: Leave him alone!

TITO: Help!

SAUNDERS: I just want to talk to you!

JULIA: Tito, you promised!

BELLHOP: Leave that man alone!

*(*MARIA, DIANA *and* MAGGIE *have by now entered the sitting room to see what's going on)*

MARIA: Tito!

TITO: Maria! *(He runs to her)* Oh, Maria! Get me outa here! Please!

MARIA *(wheeling on* DIANA *and* MAGGIE*)*: So! You make a–fun of me, eh?! You tell a–me lies!

SAUNDERS: What are you two doing here?

MAGGIE: Well—

DIANA: We were passing by, so we stopped in.

MAGGIE: To get his autograph.

BELLHOP: Did you get it?

MAGGIE: We sure did.

MARIA *(to* TITO): They told a–me you were locked in the bathroom.

JULIA: The bathroom?

MARIA: They make a–me think you were fooling around!

TITO: Maria? Me?!

DIANA: We didn't say that.

MAGGIE: Of course not.

DIANA: We were standing here, waiting for Tito—

MAGGIE: And—and—and somebody ran in there—

DIANA: Who sort of . . . looked like Tito.

MAGGIE: Right.

JULIA: Oh my God. It's the lunatic! It must be!

MAGGIE: Ahhhh–h–h–h!

MARIA: Luna–what?

JULIA: Lunatic. A madman. He's running around the city pretending he's your husband. And apparently he's violent. He actually hit a policeman!

TITO: No!

JULIA: Yes! We should call the police.

SAUNDERS: Julia—

JULIA: He could be dangerous, Henry!

SAUNDERS: Oh I doubt that—

BELLHOP: Well?! Let's see who it is!

SAUNDERS: Stay out of this!

MARIA: He's right, eh? I wanna see this a–lunatic. Maria want to see 'im!

(She walks into the bedroom, followed by the others, who speak simultaneously)

SAUNDERS: I really wouldn't bother—

DIANA: It's hardly important—

MAGGIE: Who cares who it is!

JULIA: I still think we should call the police!

SAUNDERS: Julia!

MARIA *(at the bathroom door, hollering):* Hello?! Who's in there?! *(No response.* MARIA *bangs on the door)* Come outa there! You hear me?!

BELLHOP: This–is–the–police! Come–out–with–your–hands–up!

(They all look at him. He looks behind himself and shrugs)

MARIA: I'm gonna give you three numbers! One! . . . Two! . . .

(The door unlocks . . . then opens. MAX *emerges—himself again. His make–up is washed off, and he wears white tie and tails)*

MAX: Did I miss something?

BELLHOP: It's Max.

MAGGIE *(shocked, sitting down on the bed):* Max?

SAUNDERS: Max! What a surprise!

MARIA: He doesn't even look a–like Tito!

MAX: Hi, Tito! You look great!

TITO: Max! My friend! They drive a–me crazy! You done know!

MAX: Gee, I'm sorry.

TITO: Maria, please! Take a–me home! Anyplace! Just get a–me outa here!!

MARIA: I take care, eh? Maria, she takes a–care.

TITO: *Bellezza.*

MARIA: *Carissimo.*

TITO: *Mia vongole.*

MARIA: Let's go!

JULIA: Wait! Tito!

MARIA *(to* TITO*)*: We go to Greece, eh?

TITO: Greece. That's a–good. I take a rest.

JULIA: Tito, you promised!

MARIA: Leave him alone!

JULIA, SAUNDERS & BELLHOP: Right!

*(*JULIA, SAUNDERS *and the* BELLHOP *retreat into the sitting room, followed by* MARIA *and* DIANA*)*

MAX: 'Bye, Tito.

TITO: Max. Thanks a–for everything, eh?

MAX: Take care of yourself.

TITO: And done forget. You gotta say "I'm a–the best. I'm a–Max."

MAX & TITO *(together)*: "I sing good!"

MARIA *(at the sitting room/corridor door)*: Tito! Let's a–go!

TITO: Maria. My love.

(TITO *joins* MARIA *at the door and they exit*)

JULIA: Wait! *(She hurries to the door)* Just five minutes, that's all I need! *(She exits, running. From offstage)* Tito! Please!

(Pause)

SAUNDERS: Well, I guess that's that. Everything seems to be in order now.

(MAX *and* MAGGIE *are next to each other. She looks at him in shock and confusion, realizing that she slept with him. He smiles, enjoying it)*

MAX: Yeah.

MAGGIE: Just . . . fine. (MAX *and* MAGGIE *join the others in the sitting room.* SAUNDERS *looks at* MAGGIE—*and suddenly recognizes her dress. He examines one of the sleeves)* Is anything wrong?

SAUNDERS: I'll speak to you later, young lady. You don't think I believe that story about the autograph, do you?

(The BELLHOP *has by now picked up a piece of paper from the coffee table)*

BELLHOP *(reading)*: "To Maggie. A very special person, and beautiful to look at. Merelli."

SAUNDERS *(snatching the paper)*: Let me see that!

BELLHOP: I wish I'd gotten one.

MAX: You still might catch him.

BELLHOP: Do you think so?!

MAX: It's worth a try.

BELLHOP *(bolting out of the room and down the corridor):* Mister Merelli! Mister Merelli!!

MAGGIE *(taking her autograph from* SAUNDERS*):* I'll take that, thank you.

SAUNDERS *(puzzled):* Yes, of course.

(During the following, MAGGIE *stares at the paper, lost in thought)*

DIANA: Henry, is there any food left downstairs?

SAUNDERS: I should think so.

DIANA: Good. Let's go. For some reason, *(looking at* MAX*)* I'm very hungry. *(She takes* SAUNDERS' *arm. He beams)*

SAUNDERS: Oh. Well, what a lovely idea.

(They head for the door)

MAX: Sir? Shall we say tomorrow morning? Ten o'clock. Your office.

SAUNDERS: Max—

MAX: You see, I've got some new ideas for next season.

SAUNDERS: Max!

MAX: *Carmen, La Boheme.* Then finish off with something lighter—

SAUNDERS: Like *Die Fledermaus?*

MAX: Good idea.

SAUNDERS: I'll see you in the morning. Ten–thirty.

MAX: Sir.

SAUNDERS: Max?!

MAX: Don't be late!

(Beat. SAUNDERS *is stunned. He exits, dazed.* DIANA *pauses in the doorway, gives* MAX *a look, then follows* SAUNDERS, *closing the door behind her.* MAX *and* MAGGIE *are alone. Pause)*

MAGGIE: Well . . . at least I had a fling.

MAX: Yeah.

MAGGIE: Max. I . . . I really liked it.

MAX: Me too.

MAGGIE: And I'm really glad it was with you.

MAX: Me too.

MAGGIE: But you really took an awful chance, you know, wearing his costume and making all that fuss at the stage door. And hitting a policeman! If you hadn't gotten away, you might be in prison!

MAX: Maggie—

MAGGIE: The worst part is, you didn't even get to hear him sing. And he was so wonderful.

MAX: Was he?

MAGGIE: Oh, Max, he was unbelievable. When he first came out, a . . . a shock went through the audience. And then he sang and . . . I know it sounds silly, but I started to cry. I couldn't help it. I guess that's why he's Tito Merelli.

MAX: Yeah.

(Music begins playing: the final orchestral moment from Act I of Otello. MAX *hears it;* MAGGIE *doesn't)*

MAGGIE: And even then I was thinking, God, where's Max? I want him to hear this. You know? I want to share this with him, and—

(MAX *kisses* MAGGIE's *palm and starts to sing. She is lulled by the music and closes her eyes)*

MAX *(singing):*
Gia la pleiade ardente al mar discende.
Vien . . . Venere splende.

(As MAX *holds the final note,* MAGGIE's *eyes snap open and her jaw drops. She realizes at last)*

MAGGIE: Oh, *Max!!*

(She throws her arms around him and they kiss. Bells peal out loudly through the final orchestral swell as . . .)

The curtain falls

Curtain Call

In the London and New York productions, the play proper was followed by an elaborate curtain call of sorts—that is, the actors pantomimed the entire action of the play in eighty-five seconds to the music of the Finale to Jacques Ibert's *Divertissement*. (*Divertissement* was written by Ibert in 1930 as incidental music for Labiche's farce, "Un Chapeau de Paille d'Italie." The music is therefore not only the right length but also superbly frantic. It's also generally available on record.)

A scenario describing the action of the curtain call is set forth below. The action is divided into numbered paragraphs for the sake of convenience in rehearsal. However, the action is intended to flow continuously from beginning to end without a pause, with the actors literally running from one place to the next where necessary. It's also essential that the actors use extremely broad gestures so that the story emerges as clearly (and frantically) as possible.

To avoid confusion, it should be noted that in some instances, entrances and exits occur through different doors than they do in the play proper and that, in condensing the story to eighty-five seconds, some portions of the action have been consciously omitted. A few props will have to be pre-set before the curtain call can begin. However, the curtain call should explode into action as soon as possible after the play is ended.

Finally, the director should feel free to change the action of the curtain call, where necessary, to reflect any business that may have been added to the particular production. Thus, the curtain calls in London and New York differed slightly in detail.

Scenario

1. Max and Maggie are onstage in the sitting room. Maggie, on the pouf, swoons with pleasure (thereby cueing the start of

the music). Max answers the phone and reacts to Saunders'
yell; and Saunders walks in from the corridor.

2. Saunders points at Maggie, then at the door (telling her to
   leave). Maggie walks through the connecting door and
   straight into the closet.

3. Max and Saunders hear the phone. Max answers it, indicates
   that it's Tito and hangs up. Saunders opens the sitting room/
   corridor door and the Merellis walk in. Tito of course is still
   dressed as Otello from the end of the play, but he has his
   topcoat over his shoulders at the moment.

4. Tito and Maria sling their wraps at Max, as the Bellhop enters
   the bedroom from the corridor and throws his arms up, singing.

5. Max hands the wraps to the Bellhop at the connecting door.
   The Bellhop opens the closet door and throws the wraps in to
   Maggie. Then he exits into the corridor.

6. Meanwhile, Tito and Maria argue. Then Maria stalks into the
   bedroom and straight into the bathroom, slamming the door.

7. Saunders picks up the phone and screams. He slams down
   the phone and walks out.

8. Tito and Max "shake" themselves, then sing, arms out. Then
   each picks up a wine glass and stirs the other's drink with his
   finger.

9. Maria emerges from the bathroom, making her farewell gesture. Then she walks to the closet, opens the door, sees Maggie and stifles a growl. Maria stalks out into the corridor,
   followed by Maggie.

10. Tito staggers into the bedroom, picks up the farewell note,
    screams and collapses onto the bed. Max heads for the bed-
    room. As he passes the corridor door, Diana enters, gives Max
    a kiss and exits. Then Max enters the bedroom as Saunders
    enters the bedroom from the corridor.

11. Max points at Tito ("He's dead!") and Saunders climbs onto the bed and starts shaking the corpse. Saunders then pulls an Otello wig from a hidden spot (perhaps the night table), throws it at Max and points to the bathroom.

12. Max reacts with horror, then exits into the bathroom, as Saunders walks to the sitting room/corridor door and opens it. Julia and the Bellhop enter. Saunders grabs the Bellhop by the lapels and Maggie rushes into the sitting room from the corridor, holding the rose.

13. Saunders, Maggie, Julia and the Bellhop chase around the sofa, halt for the Bellhop's flash picture, then continue the chase, as Max enters (in the Otello wig) from the bathroom. He walks to the upstage "wall" dividing the two rooms, looks at the audience and shrugs, then steps through the wall.

14. Maggie hands Max the rose. He indicates that he'll do the opera, and everyone (except Max) registers elation.

15. Everyone in the sitting room exits into the corridor, as Tito gets up from the bed. He walks into the sitting room and sits on the sofa. Simultaneously, Max enters the bedroom from the corridor, discovers that Tito's gone and runs back out the same door.

16. Julia walks into the sitting room from the corridor and frightens Tito. He ushers her back out into the corridor, then walks into the bedroom—as Max enters the sitting room from the corridor.

17. Immediately, Maggie enters the sitting room from the kitchenette and Diana enters the bedroom from the bathroom. They push the men onto the sofa and bed, respectively.

18. Maggie goes back into the kitchenette and Diana stands back to allow Tito to bound to his feet. As Max works on opening the champagne, Tito enters the sitting room, sees Max, reacts, then runs out the sitting room/corridor door.

19. Diana, hard on Tito's heels, enters the sitting room as Maggie reenters the sitting room from the kitchenette. They both discover Max at same time, and all three react.

20. Maggie and Diana chase Max through the bedroom to the bathroom door. Max exits into the bathroom, closing the door before they can catch him. As soon as Max slams the door, Maria enters the bedroom from the corridor.

21. Maggie and Diana point to the bathroom. Maria bangs on the door as Tito, Saunders, Julia and the Bellhop run into the sitting room and then into the bedroom, where they see the three women and stop.

22. Maria hits the bathroom door again, and Max strolls out of the bathroom (without his Otello wig). He gestures "What's the matter?" Shock from the others.

23. Everyone exits except Max and Maggie: Maria, Tito and Saunders go through the sitting room and out the sitting room/corridor door, as Julia, the Bellhop and Diana exit through the bedroom/corridor door. Max and Maggie simultaneously walk into the sitting room.

24. Max throws his arms up, singing. Maggie cries "Max!" and they kiss.

Blackout.

(Traditional curtain calls now follow)